BY ARTHUR J. BECKHARD

By Arthur J. Beckhard

© 2018 Jenny Phillips

goodandbeautiful.com

First Published in 1957

Cover Design by Elle Staples

Cover Illustration by Dan Burr

Punctuation has been updated to modern usage.

Black Hawk

Although Black Hawk came from a long line of warriors, he hated killing and scalping; yet his unquestioned courage and fine generalship against marauding tribes won him the title of "Chief." As head of the Sauk and the Fox, he was fired upon during peace negotiations—and so started the ill-fated Black Hawk War. Ultimately, this great-hearted leader conquered his enemies with a pen! In his autobiography, Black Hawk justifies the actions that gave him the reputation of a bloodthirsty savage, but there is also evidence that he was a reluctant warrior who spent his life in vain attempts to protect his people not only from the whites but from themselves.

TO
Evelyn and Sigmund S. Weiss, their children,
grandchildren, relatives and in-laws

TABLE OF CONTENTS

CHAPTER 1 1
CHAPTER 2 7
CHAPTER 3 12
CHAPTER 4 18
CHAPTER 5 26
CHAPTER 6 35
CHAPTER 7 43
CHAPTER 8 51
CHAPTER 9 59
CHAPTER 10 68
CHAPTER 11 76
CHAPTER 12 85
CHAPTER 13 94
CHAPTER 14 105
CHAPTER 15 111
CHAPTER 16 119
CHAPTER 17 126
CHAPTER 18 138
CHAPTER 19 146
CHAPTER 20 155
CHAPTER 21 165
CHAPTER 22 174
Appendix. *181*
Bibliography. *182*

CHAPTER 1

An arrow quivered in the trunk of the slender birch tree, just outside a small black smudge that served the two Indian boys as a target.

"Not good enough," the taller one said.

"Just because you're Black Hawk, son of Pyesa, Chief of the Sauks and the Foxes, you think—"

"Watch this, Watassa," young Black Hawk interrupted. He strung his arrow and pulled the bowstring taut. When he released it, the arrow stood in the very center of the target.

A partridge darted out of the underbrush, flying upward. Quickly both boys aimed and shot, but the bird flew away unharmed. At that moment, there was the twang of another bow, and the bird dropped fifty paces away.

They heard a laugh and saw a girl walking toward them. Although her shiny black hair was held in place by a band of brilliant blue beads and her doeskin smock elaborately decorated, her wide grin made her seem like a boy.

"Singing Bird!" Black Hawk exclaimed. "What are you doing here?"

"You should be helping with the spring plowing, not chasing after us, even though Black Hawk is your hero," Watassa said.

"You're just angry because I hit the bird you missed, Brother. Come, Black Hawk, let's find it. You can share it with us, if you're not too proud to eat something a girl killed."

"I'm not too proud," Black Hawk said. "But how did you come upon us so quietly?"

"I'm learning to walk the trails as the warriors do."

"Your brother is right," Black Hawk protested. "You should be cooking and plowing and tanning the hides of the wolf and fox so that your men may have food and clothes."

They had come out into a little clearing. Far below, on the distant plain, lay their village, Sauk-e-nong, "The Home of the Sauks," which white men called "Saukenuk." In this year of 1781, it was the largest Indian village in the whole country. Thousands of members of the Sauk tribe lived there in tipis and wickiups surrounding a Long House made of interlaced branches and mud. Across the Rock River lay the Fox village, part of Saukenuk since the tribes were united under one chief, Black Hawk's father.

They stared proudly down at their village. "It's no wonder we've sworn to defend it against all intruders," Black Hawk said.

Suddenly all about them rang the war whoops of attacking Indians, and four warriors dropped from the trees above them. Black Hawk's arms were pinioned behind him. The girl was swept from his side. A hand rose, and sunlight glinted on the blade of a long knife it held. Using the man holding him as a lever, Black Hawk swung his legs in a mighty kick. One foot caught the girl's attacker in the chest, while his other foot kicked the knife out of the attacker's hand. Then he was pulled back by his captors as one of them sank to the ground.

Watassa's arrow had found its mark. Now he closed in with a spear and knife as the fallen warrior rose and plunged toward Black Hawk.

The fight that followed was silent and deadly. Black Hawk saw that their opponents were the wily Chippewas, who neither showed nor expected mercy.

Singing Bird, crouched behind the bushes, planned to slip back to the village for help. But one of the warriors, discerning her purpose, plunged through the underbrush in pursuit.

Black Hawk, engaged in fierce hand-to-hand combat, could not help her. But Watassa flung a rock at the Chippewa, which struck him behind the ear, and he fell dead. Black Hawk somehow freed his right arm and whipped his knife into play as Singing Bird fled, running fast.

He noticed that his opponent wore a necklace of bear claws. That meant he was the son of a chief and had won the right to wear the totem of his father's clan. Also, it meant he had killed and scalped at least one opponent—a distinction Black Hawk had not yet won.

The young brave flung himself free as Black Hawk's knife flashed down so that the wound inflicted was only a surface one. The Chippewa leaped for Black Hawk's throat. But Black Hawk chopped a vicious uppercut to his jaw, and he went down. Picking up his fallen knife, Black Hawk stood over his fallen foe.

"Kill me," the youth said fearlessly.

Black Hawk looked quickly at Watassa, whose man was dead. He had no desire, however, to kill just for the sake of killing. He sheathed his knife.

"Get up," he said. "You are my prisoner."

"Kill me," the Chippewa boy said again. "I am Mowambee—Grey Owl—a chief's son."

"You have fought well and fairly," Black Hawk said. "We Sauks have the privilege of allowing a worthy enemy to live and to make him a son or a brother. I have no brother. I will have the Council make you my brother."

Slowly the young Chippewa arose. "So be it," he said solemnly. "I shall follow you throughout life. I am your brother." He hesitated, then added, "I hope I may also be your friend."

Watassa joined them, carrying the scalp-lock he had cut from his defeated enemy. Silently the three walked toward home.

That night, War Chief Pyesa and White Cloud, the Peace Chief of the Sauk, stood on the mound at the end of a long, rectangular clearing surrounded by the wigwams of the Sauk families. Opposite them was the Long House where the Council met. In the center, a great bonfire roared.

Around the fire danced Black Hawk and Watassa, while fifty drums beat out the cadence. The firelight gleamed on the faces of the watchers. The boys were appealing to all the inhabitants to be admitted as braves.

"What brave deeds have you done to deserve being called braves?" one spectator asked.

Both boys pantomimed the action of the fight that had taken place on the hill that afternoon. They were not very good actors, but luckily Singing Bird had told how brave her brother and Black Hawk had been. When the dance was over, everyone cheered to show they wanted them to become braves.

Black Hawk and Watassa walked down the length of the field to where their fathers stood with the other councilors.

"We are braves now, Father," Watassa said. And White Cloud smiled proudly.

"I understand you have chosen the breast feathers of the robin as your totem," Pyesa said.

"Yes," Watassa replied. "I wish to change my name to Red Bird."

"Here is your totem," Pyesa answered, handing him the robin feathers. "And, because you have a scalp at your belt, you may also wear the feathers of the great eagle."

"Thank you, Chief Pyesa," Red Bird said.

"You, my son," Pyesa said to Black Hawk, "may not wear eagle feathers until you have scalped an enemy. Until you do, you must wear only your totem—the tail feathers of the sparrow hawk. As the bird is black, you shall still be known as Black Hawk. When you scalp an enemy, you may change your name."

"I shall always bear the name you gave me, Father," Black Hawk answered. "I want to make it a name our people will remember. I want to make you proud of me. When may I lead a party of braves against the Sioux?"

Pyesa's eyes twinkled, but he answered solemnly, "You need more than bravery to be a leader. It will take some time to learn. After all, not two hundred full moons have passed over your head. Be patient."

"And much less solemn," said the voice of Singing Bird, who had joined them. "Chief Pyesa, Father, there is to be dancing in the Long House to celebrate the two new braves. Can't the boys come now?"

"They may," White Cloud promised. "Let us all go to the Long House."

"Take your brother and go, Singing Bird," Pyesa said. "I want to speak to my son first."

As the others went toward the Long House, Pyesa said, "I wanted to ask you about your prisoner. Young Grey Owl is the son of a Chippewa chief—not a head man nor a medicine man, but still a chief. Do you think it was wise to make him your brother?"

"Yes," Black Hawk answered. "He fought well. He is brave. He did not plead for his life. It seemed senseless to kill him."

"You knew that if you killed him and brought in his scalp, you'd have been entitled to wear the feathers of the great eagle?"

"Yes, I knew. I even thought I might not be accepted as a brave."

"I'm not sure you acted wisely, Black Hawk. I do not want my son to shrink from killing."

"I will not shrink when it is necessary, Father."

"Who can say when it is necessary?" his father demanded. "I do not want my son to grow up to be a sentimental old woman."

Black Hawk's eyes flashed angrily. "I thought we killed and took scalps to protect ourselves and our land. Also because the Great Spirit teaches that an un-scalped enemy can keep one of our people from entering the Happy Hunting Ground. But if one can make a friend out of an enemy, there is no need."

"The Chippewa may soon be at war with us," Pyesa said sternly. "Who can say whether the son of the Chippewa chief will fight with or against us?"

"Grey Owl is my brother," Black Hawk answered. "I have given him my promise. I can't go back on my word."

Pyesa was secretly pleased that the boy had the courage to stand up for his convictions. He raised a hand, and one of the runners, who stood in constant readiness near their chief, hurried to him.

"Have my son's prisoner brought to me in the wickiup next to the Long House." To Black Hawk he said, "I shall interview this young man in the small council chamber."

CHAPTER 2

"If I seem severe," Pyesa said, as they walked across the tremendous square that formed the center of Saukenuk, "it is because big trouble lies ahead for the Sauk and the Fox. The white men fight among themselves. From what our runners say, it seems that the colonists, called 'Americans,' will try to persuade the Sioux, the Chippewa, and the Osage to fight against us, if we side with the English."

"Why should we fight on either side?" Black Hawk asked.

"If we don't, they will set up forts, refuse us credit, and force us to give up our land."

Black Hawk was silent, thinking this unjust.

They entered the wickiup, and Pyesa seated himself, beckoning to his son to stand behind him. A voice called from the outside. Pyesa bade the guard enter with his prisoner.

The prisoner faced Pyesa courageously. The old chief looked at him thoughtfully, liking what he saw. "You are Mowambee—the Grey Owl?" he asked.

"I am." The boy spoke with pride and dignity, but no arrogance. Then, as Pyesa gazed at him in silence, he burst out defiantly, "Let the torture start! I shall not cry for mercy."

"Sit down," Pyesa ordered. Grey Owl gazed at him in surprise. Was this a trick? He had never heard of sitting in the presence of a victorious enemy! Cautiously, he advanced and dropped cross-legged on the buffalo robe.

"There will be no torture," Pyesa said grimly. "The Sauk and the Fox do not believe in torturing an enemy. Why did you think we would torture you?"

"The Sauk and the Fox torture more horribly than any other tribe, as is well known among our people. So we are taught to take a Sauk brave by surprise and attack without warning. We know it is better to be dead than to be their prisoner."

"There is no truth in what you have been told," Pyesa said.

"I am not to have my feet burned? You will not push the quill of the porcupine under my thumbnail?" the boy asked incredulously.

"No," Pyesa said.

Black Hawk shuddered. He had never heard of such horrible customs.

"Perhaps the Sioux and the Chippewa do such things," continued Pyesa. "The Great Spirit taught us differently. You will not be tortured. But you may be killed."

Black Hawk took a step forward. "Father," he said, "I gave my word—"

Pyesa held up his hand for silence and continued to question Grey Owl. "If need arose, would you fight for us against your own people?"

"I should never raise a hand against my father or his people," Grey Owl said.

"Then you must die," Pyesa said.

"But, for sparing my life, I should never allow anyone, even one of my family, to harm Black Hawk, who has named me his brother, or you, if you accept me as a son," Grey Owl added.

"It's as I said, Father," Black Hawk said. "He is brave and honest and speaks only the truth when it would be far easier to lie. I will be his sponsor to the Sauk tribe. Should Grey Owl betray us, my life will be forfeited."

Pyesa looked at his son. "So, if your judgment is at fault, I shall have not only a betrayal to explain to my people but a dead son to cheer me in my old age!"

"Father, you have often said that leadership requires more than courage or skill with the bow and the knife. You have said that judgment and the ability to make decisions are an even greater part of being a Chief. If I am to follow in your footsteps, my medicine must be good. My thinking must be right. I ask you to test my judgment now."

Pyesa looked from one to another, and again he felt pride because of the eagerness and honesty he saw in their faces.

"Very well," he said at last. "I am willing to test your judgment, Black Hawk, and your loyalty, Grey Owl. As my father, Thunder, used to say, 'Understanding is the enemy of hatred.' So perhaps if you two braves will trust each other and discuss the customs of our two tribes, you may learn to understand."

"I will listen and try to understand," Grey Owl said.

"And now I shall take you to the Long House and show you how we celebrate the admission of a new brave to the ranks of our warriors," Pyesa said. "Come."

As he lifted the heavy doeskin flap of the wickiup, Black Hawk turned to his father. "Thanks to you," he said, "and to the Great Spirit for giving me a wise father!"

"I can't go to a celebration like this, can I, brother Black Hawk?" Grey Owl indicated his almost total lack of covering.

"My clothes should fit you," Black Hawk said, and he led the way to his own tipi, which adjoined his father's wickiup. There he unfolded the buffalo skin that made his bed and pulled out from beneath it fringed deerskin chaps like those he had donned for his firelight dance in the square. He tossed them to Grey Owl, who thrust his long, muscular legs into them. They fit him perfectly.

While the boy was washing himself with the icy water from the goatskin bag hanging on the center pole of the wickiup, Black Hawk found a rabbit's foot brush and some powdered pigment made from the quartz and mica from the rocks on the nearby hills.

"Sit there," he commanded. "I'll paint your face so that everyone will know you are my brother."

Grey Owl, his body glistening from rubbing, sat cross-legged while Black Hawk painted three white stripes across his nose and cheeks.

"Why are you making my stripes white when yours are yellow?" Grey Owl asked. "I thought we—"

"Be quiet! How can I paint your face when your mouth is moving? All the boys of the Sauk and Fox nation are divided into two teams so that we may be rivals in games and contests."

"I thought I was to fight with you, and for you, as your brother," Grey Owl said later as they left the wickiup and started running toward the Long House. "I thought I'd be on your team."

"We fight each other as brothers," Black Hawk answered. "But as brothers we fight together against any outsider who threatens our people or our land."

As they entered, they discovered that the celebration had barely reached its peak. Eight painted, grinning braves were beating out a blood-pounding rhythm on tall catskin drums. Four more were blowing through flute-like reeds. Red Bird was dancing in the center of the earthen floor, illustrating the many brave deeds he planned in what seemed like a fierce and blood-curdling career.

A shout greeted Black Hawk's entrance, for he was one of the two guests of honor. When Red Bird danced over to the entrance, flinging himself at Black Hawk's feet, the shout grew into a roar.

Black Hawk raised his friend from the floor and flung an arm around his perspiring shoulders. His other arm he threw around Grey Owl, and the three faced their friends in a demonstration of loyalty.

Singing Bird ran up to greet them. "I see now why you were in such a hurry to get here," Grey Owl said, and Singing Bird's eyes crinkled in a smile at his flattery.

She had always grinned like a boy, but Grey Owl's words had brought a different kind of smile to her face. Black Hawk wasn't sure he liked it.

"Do you know the wind dance?" she asked Grey Owl.

"I know it as my people—" He stopped and corrected himself. "As the people with whom I grew up taught me."

"Will you show me?" Singing Bird asked.

Grey Owl started to answer, then paused and looked at Black Hawk, who hesitated only an instant. He smiled at both of them and dropped his arm from Grey Owl's shoulder.

As Grey Owl walked onto the center of the floor and Singing Bird stood gazing after him, Black Hawk wondered if it might not have been wiser to have his newly adopted brother on his own team instead of a rival.

CHAPTER 3

In the weeks that followed, Black Hawk wondered if Grey Owl would ever stop asking questions.

"Why is this land so important to the Sauk and the Fox?" he asked as the two boys were returning to the great village from a hunting trip in the hills. "There is so much land—such never-ending forests and waters. There is plenty of game to give everyone food. Why can't other tribes hunt here, too?"

"This land is ours. It was so designated by the Great Spirit," Black Hawk answered. "When my people lived among the French in the land called Quebec in Canada, the land along the Tumbling Waters, what the French called the Saint Lawrence River, belonged to us. Then the Great Spirit appeared to my great-grandfather, Men-Em-Sha, and bade him make a long journey, and at the end, he found the man he had been told would be there. This man, Prince Philippe, told him if he would call upon the Fox to join the Sauk and lead both tribes out of Canada into the Valley of the Father of Waters, the French would give them all this land on which to live to the end of time."

"Was your great-grandfather Chief of the Sauk?"

"No," Black Hawk replied. "He had not even won his eagle feathers. He told the son of the French king this, and said he did not know if his people would follow him, and that he must seek advice from the Great Spirit. So the French white man had to wait while my great-grandfather went alone into the deep woods and asked for help. Again the Great Spirit appeared to him and bade him go back home and call both tribes together and tell them he had been ordered to take over the position of chief of both tribes and to lead them out of Canada."

"And what happened?" Grey Owl asked.

"The whites were angry at the delay but agreed to meet again with my great-grandfather twelve dawns later. So he went back, called together both tribes, and told them of his vision and his meeting with the white prince. The Chief of the Sauk was not happy about this. He had been a chief for a long time. His followers were angry that a young brave dared ask to be chief in his stead. As the men muttered that such impertinence should be punished by death, a thunderstorm appeared. My great-grandfather said this was a sign that the Great Spirit was angry because his people were not obeying his orders."

"And they believed him?"

"Just at that moment, a bolt of lightning struck the bear totem in the center of the square, and it caught fire. My great-grandfather pointed to it and said nothing. The crowd began to chant. The older Chief took off his headdress of eagle feathers, and the Medicine Man handed him the otterskin, insignia of the medicine man. And they agreed to follow him."

"Your great-grandfather had courage," Grey Owl said.

"My father says he was a very shrewd young man," Black Hawk answered. "At any rate, they renamed him Thunder, Son-of-the-Lightning, and he met with the whites and made his finger mark on a paper which gave us all these lands forever. And all the Sauk and the Fox have sworn always to defend them, since that was the will of the Great Spirit."

"Or your great-grandfather," Grey Owl suggested.

"You are right," Black Hawk admitted. "It is possible that my great-grandfather willed it so. Just as it is possible that one of the

Sioux or Osage or Chippewa so willed it and claimed it to be the will of the Great Spirit. But surely the Great Spirit cannot have told all tribes the land was theirs!"

"Perhaps the Great Spirit meant for us to defend the land from the whites," Scowling Wolf, Red Bird's brother, who was with them, said.

"That could not be," Black Hawk answered. "It was the whites who gave it to us. Surely they would not take it away. The French have always been our friends. French traders come to give us the things we need for hunting. Then, in the spring, they buy our furs."

As they reached the cliff that overlooked Saukenuk, they saw signs of great activity. They ran down to learn what was going on and were told that runners had come with the message that a large band of Chippewa had been sighted hunting buffalo in the plains belonging to the Sauk. Raiding parties were being formed to chase away the trespassers.

Black Hawk sought out his father, who was issuing orders in the Long House.

"Father," he said, "have I your permission to lead a band in the attack?"

Pyesa looked at him, amusement mixed with pride. "Who would be willing to risk his life under the command of an untried youth of barely sixteen summers?"

"I think I can find ten who would."

"Who can tell whether you have the judgment, the calmness under stress, to be a leader? However, if there are forty men willing to place themselves at your command, I shall not stand in your way."

"When do we leave?"

"All parties must be ready to leave an hour before dawn tomorrow."

"We'll be there," Black Hawk said confidently. But his confidence was soon shaken, for he found no one wanted to go with a boy who had not earned a single scalp.

Finally, he sought Red Bird. "Since your father is a Peace Chief, you do not have to fight," Black Hawk said. "But you are brave. Will you serve under me?"

"Of course."

"We must find thirty-eight others to go with us."

"There's Scowling Wolf, for one," Red Bird said. "Although he's only thirteen, he has friends."

"Your brother is at your service." It was Grey Owl, who had come up quietly.

"What about Howling Coyote?" Red Bird asked. "Let me do the recruiting. We'll report to you at the Long House by nightfall."

Black Hawk and Grey Owl went to their tipi and began readying their gear. Their preparations were complete, but there was still no word from Red Bird.

At last Scowling Wolf brought a message. "My brother says to tell you Howling Coyote will go only if he can command his followers. There are forty who will go if he does, but Red Bird wasn't sure how you would feel about it."

"Very well," Black Hawk answered. "I shall lead the others. Howling Coyote can command his own followers."

Without a word, Scowling Wolf disappeared in the darkness. Then Black Hawk went to report to Chief Pyesa. There was excited activity at the Long House as the various groups assembled. As Chief of All the Sauk and the Fox, Pyesa issued final commands to the leaders, who then rejoined their own bands.

Black Hawk stood in the shadows for several moments before he spoke to his father. Eager and excited as he was, he choked up suddenly with pride in Chief Pyesa, respected and obeyed by all. He had a great desire to win his praise and see his eyes light up with pride in him. And he was fifteen and had never killed a man! He was determined not to fail his father's faith in him.

At last Black Hawk stepped forward. "Father," he said, "forty braves are ready to leave with me before dawn."

Pyesa turned to him in surprise and sadness. This was his only son. He had not expected Black Hawk to meet the conditions he had imposed. But, after a brief moment, he forced himself to forget that he was this boy's father.

"You will lead your squad to the south," he said.

Black Hawk looked at him in surprise. He had heard the others being ordered to the north and west.

"It has been reported that there are more than five hundred of the enemy," Pyesa said. "A band of forty, no matter how brave, would have little chance against so large a force. Therefore, you will go south. You will find those who have escaped our arrows and spears. They will be traveling homeward in small, weary groups encumbered by their buffalo meat."

"But, Father," Black Hawk protested, "we want to make you proud."

"It takes as much courage to attack fifty men as five hundred," Pyesa said.

He smiled at his son, and Black Hawk felt a great warmth toward the chieftain.

"We shall bring home buffalo meat as well as scalps," he said.

So, in the dim gray light of early morning his band assembled. The mist rose as Black Hawk took his place in front of his party. Before him stood Howling Coyote, who had brought his thirty older braves. A little to his right were Red Bird and Grey Owl, heading nine young men. As Black Hawk looked at his group, he felt a sudden moment of fear and great loneliness. Then he pulled himself together.

Suddenly there was the whoosh of many moccasined feet as the women ran out to say goodbye to their men, and Black Hawk found himself looking down into Singing Bird's earnest face.

"Wear this," she commanded, handing him a wrought silver armband with a turquoise stone at its center. "It was not easy to carve. See, it has the sparrow hawk on it. Wear it bravely."

Before he could thank her, she had turned away.

"Grey Owl," she called, and the boy almost leapt to her side. "Here is one for you. It is just like Black Hawk's. I made them both for him, but you are his brother. It is right that you both be equal halves of one whole."

Black Hawk frowned. He had grown up with Singing Bird. She did most things as well as he did. Sometimes he had resented it, but, after all, she was his friend, not Grey Owl's. Angrily he turned away and faced the men.

"Warriors! Face the rising sun!" he cried. And, turning eastward, he raised both arms in supplication toward the warming, fortune-bringing sun, which was just showing beyond the encircling hills. After a few moments, he dropped his arms to his sides. The others followed his example.

"Now, follow me!" Black Hawk cried, and ran with long, loping strides toward the south.

CHAPTER 4

Black Hawk assumed the advance position, known to his tribesmen as the "point," running on silent feet much faster than the pace set for his followers. Far behind him was Howling Coyote and his band, in constant readiness to receive reports relayed to them by the runners, Scowling Wolf and Grey Owl.

Black Hawk found it lonely, traveling far in advance of his band, knowing that their safety and the success of the venture depended entirely upon his skill. His thoughts kept turning to Singing Bird. Did she admire Grey Owl more than she did him? Why wouldn't she? Grey Owl had three scalps at his belt. Black Hawk had none, nor any great desire to acquire them. He knew he did not fear fighting; it was just that scalping for the sake of obtaining a trophy seemed senseless to him. But he must show Singing Bird, as well as Pyesa, that he was no coward!

It was barely past midday when the first sign of trouble appeared. It had been agreed that Red Bird would relieve Black Hawk as "point" when the sun reached its zenith. When Red Bird failed to appear, Black Hawk knew something was wrong.

He dared not pause and wait for the band to catch up to him, for the delay would mean they would not reach Wantauk-o-see, the Lake of the Crying Geese, by nightfall. He must go on.

At last he heard a twig snap, then the sound of moccasins on dirt. It was not Red Bird. He would never have snapped a twig! Black Hawk swung himself onto a low-hanging branch and waited. In a few moments Scowling Wolf appeared. He was running, his head bent low to catch the signs. Black Hawk let him pass, then dropped noiselessly from the limb onto the earth behind him.

"Scowling Wolf," he called. The boy leaped into the air, and in spite of his worry, Black Hawk could not help smiling. "You would have been killed if I had been an enemy."

"I would not!" the boy answered indignantly. "You would have left some warning sign. You are too good a point to let your followers walk into a trap."

Black Hawk's smile widened. "My thanks for your confidence." Then his smile faded. "What is wrong?" he asked. "Why has your brother not come to relieve me?"

"There is bad trouble," the boy answered. "Howling Coyote says you do not know where you are going. He has refused to follow farther. Red Bird has been trying to convince him that you are wise. He managed to keep the Coyote from leading his men toward the setting sun as he wants to do. Red Bird has persuaded them to follow at least until I return."

"And what is it they wish me to say?" Black Hawk asked.

"The Coyote gives you little choice. I am to tell you to return with me and take your warriors with his toward where they will join the others who went before, or else go on alone."

Black Hawk frowned. To go alone meant certain death. To return meant an admission of failure.

"Tell the Coyote," he said, "that we shall reach the Lake of the Crying Geese before the dew falls. Once there, we can camp for the night. Tell him that only a little way from the lake is a canyon which has long been dry, that if he *must* join the others, he can best do so by walking the basin of the canyon. It will lead him directly and safely to the great plains where the buffalo graze. Tell him, also, that if he does not bring his followers to the lake, he will be responsible for the death of the son of Pyesa, Chief of All the Sauk and the Fox.

Tell him I am going on!"

He raised his hand in the age-old signal of dismissal and farewell. The boy looked at him admiringly. Then he, too, raised his arm straight over his head and started at a loping run in the direction from which he had come.

Without a backward glance, Black Hawk resumed his journey, carefully breaking twigs or marking a tree trunk whenever there would be doubt as to the trail. He dared not think of the disgrace that would follow if his challenge was not accepted.

It was dusk by the time he emerged from the forest to behold the mirror-like surface of the Lake of the Crying Geese, in a valley surrounded by gently sloping hills.

He went down to the shore and drank thirstily. To give himself something to do while waiting in nervous uncertainty for the arrival of his followers, he looked for a good location for the camp. He cut twigs with his knife and dragged larger branches for the fire.

At last he heard a soft whisper of sound from the woods behind him. It took willpower not to give a whoop of triumph and relief, but he managed to go on about the business of building the fire in silence and pretended to be calm.

And, like shadows, the others came. In silence they went to the lakeshore and drank.

Only Red Bird, Grey Owl, and Scowling Wolf stopped for a moment by his side.

"They have come," Red Bird said quietly.

"Thank you," Black Hawk replied. "You have done well." Then the three boys went on down to the lake to drink and wash.

While some of the braves caught fish, others heated stones in the fire to bake the catch. But Black Hawk remained, sitting cross-legged by the fire, awaiting Howling Coyote.

Long after darkness had engulfed the valley, Howling Coyote finally deigned to approach the fire and seat himself before Black Hawk. Still no word was spoken.

"My men grow restive," the older man said at last.

"Have they no faith in the wisdom of Pyesa?" Black Hawk asked.

"They think perhaps Chief Pyesa was more the father than the warrior when he ordered his son to a place where there is no fighting," Howling Coyote replied.

"Chief Pyesa has given me a mission in which there can be much honor and many coups," Black Hawk replied.

"But not many scalps," the warrior replied.

"The scalps are less important than the recapture of our own buffalo meat and hides which have been stolen from us by the Chippewas," Black Hawk said.

"It is well known among the Sauk and the Fox that the son of their chief is not overeager to take scalps and that his spear is as naked as a newborn bird. My warriors do not share your feeling. We want to be where the fighting is thickest."

"My father's medicine has never failed his people," Black Hawk said.

"Let us not deal in anger," Howling Coyote said patronizingly. "We do not wish to offend the son of our chief, but it is within each leader's right to lead his men as he sees fit. My men and I will leave you when we reach the mouth of the canyon of which you spoke."

Black Hawk said nothing. He knew that lesser chiefs could withdraw their followers if they lacked faith in the leader of the band. He sat staring into the flames, feeling that he had failed his father. Suddenly he realized that he was also thinking of having to tell Singing Bird of his failure. Howling Coyote looked at the frowning boy and arose silently and left.

But Black Hawk still sat staring into the fire. Why should he care what a girl thought of him? He decided he would think of Singing Bird no more. In the morning he would try to persuade the braves to remain with him. Even at the risk of being thought a coward, he would not defy his father's orders and go with Howling Coyote's men to join the fighting in the north.

The shadows of the cottonwood trees were slanting across the prairie when they reached the mouth of the canyon. Black Hawk stood on a low rock, urging each warrior as he passed to stay with him. In sullen silence or with ugly sneers, they passed him and followed Howling Coyote into the narrow pass down toward the dry bed of the canyon. Not one of Howling Coyote's men stayed behind.

It was a great temptation to follow them. Howling Coyote had fourteen scalps on his spear and was known as a leader. Perhaps he was right. Certainly no one would blame Black Hawk for a change of plans. The seven young braves who remained looked hopefully at him for a sign that he had changed his mind. For a long moment he stood gazing after the disappearing strength of his command.

Then Black Hawk stepped down from the rock, swung his arm in a great arc over his head and forward, and beckoned his few loyal followers on—southward—away from the canyon's mouth.

Two nights later the almost exhausted warriors came to a hilltop and gazed with amazement and horror on a startling sight.

Pyesa had been right. The Chippewa were retreating homeward with their catch and were coming south. But either they had defeated the Sauks or else the Sauks had arrived too late, for here below them, on the great expanse of prairie, Black Hawk's little band beheld a camp of nearly a hundred warriors!

The braves had brought their squaws, and both men and women were skinning and butchering the captured buffalo. As the steaks were cut from the carcass, the women wrapped them in moistened mullein leaves and fern and tied them together with dried intestines. Then the meat was packed onto the horses, and the loaded animals were led away. Each pack animal was guarded by a brave on another horse, and at long intervals, groups of ten or twelve warriors left toward the south.

"We will wait until the last party is ready to go, then we will attack," Black Hawk said.

As night fell, they ate berries and pemmican, not daring to start a fire on the hilltop, then bedded down under the trees. But Black Hawk could not sleep. He rose and walked to the edge of the cliff overlooking the plain, watching the camp below. He noticed that the horses that were packed and ready to leave had not gone. The party was awaiting the dawn before starting for home. A daring idea struck him. He woke Red Bird and led him away from the others.

"We can cut two of the horses free. If we can do it without waking any of the warriors, we can lead the horses back up here."

Red Bird smiled for the first time since they had left Saukenuk. It was a brave, foolish thing to try—a plan after his own heart. He did all he could do to restrain a war whoop!

Without another word, the two boys ran silently down the hill to the very edge of the encampment. Then they crawled through the underbrush where the horses were tethered. Rising noiselessly, Black Hawk clapped a hand over a pinto's nose to keep it from whinnying, while Red Bird cut the rope that tied it to a stake. Silently they walked with it into the woods.

As they climbed back up the long trail through the woods, they listened tensely for some sound of an alarm, but there was none. They succeeded in getting the horse with his precious load back to their camping place.

Then Black Hawk woke the others and arranged for teams to work as he and Red Bird had done. By sunrise they had four horses hidden on the hilltop.

While they were cutting the fifth animal loose, one of the squaws wakened and saw them. She came running toward them, and Red Bird silenced her with a blow. She groaned as she fell. To keep her from being discovered, he threw her onto the horse's back, and both boys ran with the horse into the woods. But her cry had been heard. A warrior came running toward them.

"Go on with the horse," Black Hawk whispered, and he slapped the animal's flank so that it ran up the trail.

Black Hawk knew that the warrior could not see them. He dared not risk killing him for fear of awakening the whole camp. But he gripped his knife in readiness as the warrior approached, nearer and nearer to the woods. When he reached the horses, he peered down at the string of five cut rope ends hanging from their stakes and turned toward the camp. He was going to give the alarm! Black Hawk could never reach him in time to silence him.

Out of the shadows another darker shadow rose. Light caught the sheen of a flashing knife, and the enemy warrior sank to the ground without a sound. The dark shadow was Grey Owl! He had been freeing another horse with Scowling Wolf and had acted quickly. Black Hawk ran forward and grasped his arm, squeezing it to show his thanks.

Together they carried the dead warrior deep into the woods. Grey Owl scalped him, covering him with leaves so he would not be discovered till they were far away. Then he and Black Hawk ran after Red Bird.

"Is the squaw dead?" Black Hawk asked.

"No."

Black Hawk spoke to her. She said nothing, but looked at him with large eyes like those of an injured dog.

"Shall we kill her?" Red Bird asked. "It would mean a scalp..."

"No," Black Hawk decided. "I shall bring her home as a present to Singing Bird."

"Knowing my sister, I think she would prefer a scalp," Red Bird said.

Black Hawk was unable to meet Red Bird's eyes. He didn't want his friend to see that he just didn't care to kill this defenseless woman.

CHAPTER 5

Black Hawk whispered orders to destroy all traces of their camp. Then, cutting thin strips of soft hide from one of the buffalo skins, he tied them around the noses of the horses to ensure silence. Quietly they left the plateau and hurried onto the homeward trail.

At midday they reached the mouth of the canyon where Howling Coyote had left them. Black Hawk, constantly on the alert, was trailing the others. His sharp eyes detected what Red Bird and Grey Owl had missed.

"Stop!" he cried. When the others ran back, he pointed to the bushes along the trail. "Blood," he said, "and not yet dry."

He ran, crouching, along the trail, watching for more bloodstains. When he passed the horses, he searched for the story the footprints might tell him.

"See. There were two men—one, badly hurt, half-carried by the other. His right foot drags along the path, and his left one barely reaches the ground."

"They came out of this canyon," Red Bird exclaimed. "They might be friends or Chippewas."

"No way of telling," Black Hawk said. "We must move carefully. From here on, I'll take 'point.'"

The others dropped back to guard against attack from the rear. The wounded men must have had several hours' start, for there was no further sign of them all that day.

At nightfall, when they reached the shore of the Lake of the

Crying Geese, they came upon the wounded brave, delirious from pain and loss of blood.

"It's Little Beaver," Black Hawk said, "one of Howling Coyote's best braves."

The captured squaw, who had trudged uncomplainingly on the long march, knelt by the wounded brave. Carefully she removed the leather and wet mud pack that had been placed on his shattered leg, then cleaned up the deep wound and bandaged it with strips torn from her own garments.

All night the young braves tried to make the badly wounded man as comfortable as possible. They could catch only an occasional phrase he muttered which didn't make much sense.

"Big Beaver get help," he said once. And they knew his brother had gone ahead to Saukenuk.

"Help no use," he muttered later. "Watanka means us all to die."

Toward morning he said Big Beaver had gone to beg forgiveness of Pyesa for disobeying his orders. Then he kept repeating, "He turn the buffalo. The buffalo."

As the sun rose, he suddenly sat up and shouted, "The buffalo! Look! The buffalo!" Then he fell back and died.

They led a stallion over to where he lay and gently lifted his body onto its back, tying it on with thongs. Then they started on the long trail to Saukenuk. The captured squaw walked beside the horse, steadying Little Beaver's body.

Black Hawk found himself watching her. She must have slipped off to bathe during the night, for her face and hands looked clean. This surprised him, for he had been told that Chippewas were dirty. He liked the way she walked. The others seemed to like her looks, too.

Perhaps, Black Hawk thought, he had been foolish to announce he was going to give her to Singing Bird. He could keep her for himself. She was his by right of capture and because he was the leader. She could cook for him and wait upon him. She could even be his wife. After all, Sauks were permitted to have five wives. Why should he think only of Singing Bird?

Yet he knew he had always thought only of Singing Bird. All his life he had taken for granted they would always be together. He wanted no one else. But did Singing Bird feel the same way? He thought that, like his father, she wished he would take more pleasure in killing. Perhaps her brother had been right. Perhaps she would have preferred a scalp to the Chippewa squaw.

Red Bird trotted up to him and said, smiling, "Her name is Crescent Moon. Isn't that a nice name?"

Black Hawk smiled but didn't answer.

It was dusk before they approached the high mesa overlooking Saukenuk. Although tired, the thought of coming home gave them fresh energy. They were returning without the loss of a single brave. Chief Pyesa would be proud of him, Black Hawk thought.

Unexpectedly, the acrid smell of smoke stung their nostrils. They looked at each other in sudden fear. The great village of Saukenuk was on fire! The Chippewas must have defeated the Sauks and come to raid, rob, and burn their homes! The desperate need to know the worst drove them on, and they ran up the long trail to the top of the mesa.

The sight that met their eyes was such a relief that, for a moment, they forgot its sad meaning.

"It's just the funeral smudge fires!" Red Bird exclaimed.

In front of every wickiup and tipi in the great square, rows of small fires sent their plumes of smoke high into the air, to join the dark cloud that hung over the village.

"The whole band must have been wiped out!" Black Hawk cried. They all began to run, stumbling down the sloping trail.

Black Hawk's thoughts raced ahead of him. Who would be Chief of the Warriors if Pyesa had been killed? Certainly not a sixteen-year-old boy who had not taken a single scalp! A brave with no taste for killing! And Singing Bird—would she be proud of him? Or ashamed? Would she care that Grey Owl carried a scalp and he didn't?

They were halfway down the long, wide trail when Black Hawk saw her. She was waiting for them where the trail emerged from the woods.

Black Hawk summoned Grey Owl to his side. "We will go in together," he said. He wanted to learn which of them Singing Bird would run to first. But she passed both of them and threw her arms around the neck of her oldest brother.

"We thought you were all dead," she told them. "Big Beaver crawled in, badly wounded and out of his head. When Chief Pyesa tried to question him, all he could say before he died was that the whole band under Black Hawk's command had been wiped out—that it was a punishment from the Great Spirit for disobeying their leader.

"Chief Pyesa thought his son had disobeyed him and led his men into an ambush in the canyon. He has been mourning not only your death but his faith in you, Black Hawk."

"We didn't disobey him," Black Hawk told her proudly.

"Come," he said to the others. "We must report without delay."

When the villagers saw the little procession coming down the trail, there was great excitement. People ran from their tipis and the Long House to greet them.

Black Hawk took the arm of the captured squaw and presented

her to Singing Bird. Although the speech of the two women differed greatly, they seemed to understand one another. Paying no more attention to the returning warrior, Singing Bird walked, arm in arm with her new companion, as they chattered like chipmunks.

Reaching the Long House, Black Hawk, with Red Bird and Grey Owl, went in to report to his father. Chief Pyesa neither smiled nor nodded but gazed at the three young warriors with grim disapproval.

"If, as has been said, you disobeyed my command, you are not my son," Pyesa said sternly.

"Black Hawk did not disobey, Chief Pyesa," Red Bird explained. "It was only the followers of Howling Coyote."

"These two and seven others followed me and served with great loyalty and devotion," Black Hawk added quickly.

"I am glad." The great chieftain's stern mouth relaxed. "Tell me what happened."

Pyesa's eyes gleamed in anger as he heard of the ultimatum the older leader had issued on their second night out of camp. He nodded approval as he heard of his son's decision. But when Black Hawk came to the capture of Crescent Moon, Pyesa shook his head.

"So you still wear no scalp at your belt," he said sadly.

"But Father," Black Hawk protested, "there was no need for killing."

"There is always need for killing if you expect to be a leader of the Sauk men," Pyesa answered. "You are a warrior. Yet Red Bird, who is the son of the Peace Chief, has a scalp and you have none. Your adopted brother has many scalps and now has added another to grace his spear. Neither of them can become chieftain. Yet you, my son, who hope one day to become Chief of All the Sauk and the Fox, you think there is no need for killing!"

"I'm sorry that you are not pleased by our sortie."

"Oh, for an inexperienced boy, you have done well enough," his father answered. "And you have learned that leadership is more than bravery and the desire to lead. In time you could be a great leader, but not without the desire to kill. Go on with your story."

Pyesa again listened without interruption until Black Hawk described Little Beaver's delirious mutterings.

"Is that all Little Beaver said?" he asked. "'Watanka has punished us. The buffalo—the buffalo…?' You heard nothing else?"

"Nothing," Black Hawk answered, and the others nodded in agreement.

Then, for the first time since they had come before him, the young braves noticed that the lines of worry around Pyesa's mouth seemed to fade away, and he smiled. The boys sighed with relief.

"Come," Pyesa said. "Our people await us. We will have a victory dance tonight to celebrate the safe homecoming of my son and his loyal followers."

The young braves followed their leader to the little clearing space in front of the Long House, standing behind him as he raised his hand in a signal to the men and women who had gathered.

"Spread the word," Pyesa cried. "In place of the smudge fires of death will be built the great bonfire of life. For this day we have beheld a miracle. The Great Spirit has shown us his power and will. Those who disobeyed died. Those who followed their chief's orders returned. The Council will meet tonight after the fire has died down to talk over the disposal of the horses and the buffalo meat that Black Hawk brought home. Go and prepare a feast of thanksgiving."

A murmur rippled through the crowd and grew to a vast roar as the squaws went to prepare the food and the warriors to deck themselves in their best chaps and feathers.

Pyesa turned back to the boys. "Grey Owl and Red Bird, you have served my son well. Go and prepare for the dance. I want to speak to Black Hawk."

The two handsome young braves obediently ran off. Pyesa and Black Hawk returned to the Long House. Seated in front of the great hearth, father and son were silent for some time. Black Hawk wanted to ask about the battle at the hunting grounds, but Pyesa seemed to have withdrawn into a world of his own.

"My son," he said at last, "do you remember the story I've told you many times—of how your great-grandfather became the War Chief of the Sauk?"

"I remember every word," Black Hawk replied, and repeated the story he had told to Grey Owl.

"When we arrived at the hunting grounds," Pyesa said, as though in answer to Black Hawk's unspoken question, "we discovered we had been badly misinformed. There were many more Chippewas than we had expected. They outnumbered us five to one. So, under cover of darkness, I stationed braves along the top ledges of the steep wall of the Great Canyon. The Chippewas were down on the plains below, killing the grazing buffalo, skinning their kill and packing the loads onto the horses. Thinking that your band of forty braves could defeat at least a hundred because they would not be expecting attacks on their return journey, I allowed many to make off with their loaded horses. Before the sun rose, we attacked from the outer rim of the plain, making as much noise as possible. In their first surprise, the enemy did as I hoped. They rode for the corner of the canyon where they thought we would not attack them. Then our eighteen rifles and our arrows got to work."

"That was wonderful planning, Father," Black Hawk said.

"But we were not enough for them. They could have come back out of the canyon and killed us all. It was then I thought of the buffalo. We stampeded them into the canyon. The buffalo ran them down, trampled them, and kept going. Standing on the rim, we could hear the screams of the horses mingling with the death cries of the enemy and the bellowing of the buffalo. We could see nothing but clouds of dust. That was the bloody chaos that Howling Coyote's men walked into."

Black Hawk shuddered.

"I didn't know they were there until I returned home and Big Beaver muttered about the buffalo as he died. No one else heard him. No one knows how those men died. That's why I asked if anyone but you had heard his brother and what he had said. None of my warriors knows anything except that not a Chippewa returned alive from the canyon's mouth and that the only Sauks who died were those of your party."

"I begin to see," Black Hawk said gravely.

"Who can say whether the lightning struck the totem pole at that precise moment because it was the will of the Great Spirit?"

"No one could prove that this was not so," Black Hawk answered.

"There are those who might say that I killed thirty-two of our tribesmen by stampeding the buffalo into the canyon."

"No one could say that! You didn't know our braves were there!"

"Others might say *you* were responsible for their deaths because you told of the southern entrance to the canyon."

"But I didn't know—"

Pyesa held up his hand for silence and continued. "People think as they are told to think by their Chiefs and Medicine Men," he said. "And who knows? Perhaps it was the Great Spirit who caused the death of these men in order to establish you as their future leader! Are we not taught that we must have faith in the all-knowing wisdom of Watanka, the Great Spirit?"

"That is true," Black Hawk said.

"Perhaps the Great Spirit in his wisdom knows that it would be difficult for you to persuade men to follow you since you have neither killed nor scalped an enemy. Perhaps the Great Spirit believed you needed help, and so he provided a sign for every Sauk and Fox to understand. I only know that your great-grandfather pointed out the sign to his people. They believed it. I am certain that after he heard the story repeated as the telling of a miracle, he too came to believe it. It was believing it that gave him the authority, the power, and the courage to lead both great tribes out of the wilderness of Canada to this new land and to receive it as a gift forever from the white French chief. I only know that to be a great leader one must be bold. And one must remember that lightning strikes only once."

He stood up, and the boy also rose to his feet. "I no longer need the help of Watanka to make me a chief," he said. "You do."

"You are very wise, Father," Black Hawk said.

The corners of Pyesa's lips twitched into a smile. "It is a proud and happy father who can pass on his wisdom to his son," he said.

For a moment they stood looking at each other. Then Pyesa took his son's arm, and they started for the door. As Black Hawk held the flap up for Pyesa to pass, he realized suddenly that this talk was to influence his whole life.

CHAPTER 6

Pyesa's advice proved to be "good medicine." As winter approached, some of the neighboring tribes, driven by hunger, raided the Sauk hunting grounds and the forests surrounding Saukenuk. The braves flocked eagerly to Black Hawk when he called for volunteers to go on sorties against the raiders. It was believed that the Great Spirit would punish anyone who refused to heed his summons.

And truly it seemed as if the Great Spirit smiled upon Black Hawk, for his every venture was victorious! The warriors liked to follow him because he was brave and daring, and his generalship was shrewd. His counterattacks often resulted in the death and capture of many Chippewas, and even the powerful Sioux, without the loss of a single Sauk.

At first the tribe thought it strange that he never killed except in self-defense or defending one of his men. They came to accept this because it gave them greater opportunities to collect coups. And, because Black Hawk never scalped a fallen enemy, they were able to add many scalps to their own spears.

But Black Hawk was not happy. He knew Pyesa wanted his son to be a great warrior, not just a shrewd captain. Pyesa never let Black Hawk forget that killing was a part of the Indian code.

Singing Bird, too, seemed to prefer the company of Grey Owl, whose spear flaunted an imposing array of scalps. Of course, he could order Grey Owl not to see the girl, but he wanted Singing Bird to come to him of her own free will. As he was silent and awkward in her company, she turned more and more to Grey Owl for fun and companionship.

Another thing that worried him was the horses he had brought to Saukenuk. At first they aroused great interest and curiosity. But after the novelty wore off, their owners found them a luxury. As no one knew how to put them to use, the Council decided they must be killed.

On the day set for the execution, Francis St. Clair arrived in Saukenuk. He was the only white man Black Hawk had ever seen. Over the years he had often proved his genuine friendship for the Sauk and the Fox. He lived up both to the spirit and to the letter of the agreement made between the tribes and the French.

St. Clair trusted his Indian friends, and they never failed him. Every fall he provided them with traps and rifles, and each spring they paid for these supplies by bringing him the skins and meat of bear, buffalo, and deer.

But now he came for a more serious purpose. He explained to the chiefs that henceforth they would have to deal with the scarlet-coated British in Canada, because a general named Wolfe had defeated the French General Montcalm in Quebec and Montreal.

"If the English father in Canada will not give you the things you need for hunting on trust as we have done, perhaps the Spanish father in St. Louis will do so," St. Clair said. He explained that Napoleon had ceded the French rights in the Mississippi to the Spanish.

"But it is a much longer journey to St. Louis than to Canada," White Cloud protested.

"If only the Great Spirit had given you a knowledge of horses," St. Clair said, "you could pack your goods on their backs. But you have never learned to use horses as the white man does, and so the Great

Spirit has kept you without them."

Then the councilors all spoke at once. "We have horses! Black Hawk, whom Watanka favors, brought us horses!"

"Who is Black Hawk?" asked St. Clair.

"The son of Chief Pyesa."

"The Lucky One."

"The young brave all warriors follow, though he rarely kills and never scalps!"

"It is truly a sign from the Bon Dieu!" St. Clair exclaimed. "The Great Spirit wishes the Sauk and the Fox to have horses."

"Our warriors do not ride," Pyesa said firmly. "We can follow a trail faster and surprise an enemy better without the noises made by clumsy beasts."

"But you can use a horse in peacetime. A horse pulls a plow and makes a straight furrow."

"What then would our squaws do?" White Cloud asked. "Ploughing and farming are not for young braves. That is women's work."

St. Clair shrugged in helpless annoyance. Then he smiled.

"We've got along together well, all these years, *mes amis*," he said, "partly because we have not tried to change each other's ways. I shall not begin now. But I strongly urge you to go to Montreal to see your new English father. I'm afraid you'll find that the British will not supply you on trust as the French have."

"We will go," White Cloud agreed. "It is good medicine."

"Good," St. Clair said, pleased that they were not angered. Then Black Hawk stepped forward.

"And with my father's permission," he said, "I shall study the use of the horses if the Council will agree to keep them alive until the warriors return from Canada."

St. Clair looked at the tall, dark young brave and nodded approval. Then he turned to White Cloud. "You will do well to let Black Hawk study the horses and how to ride. The Great Spirit puts words in his mouth. The Sauk and the Fox will one day thank Black Hawk for bringing horses to them."

The moon had waned from full to crescent and back to full before the little party of warriors returned from Montreal with full confirmation of everything St. Clair had prophesied. By that time Black Hawk had followed the Frenchman's directions in preparing food for the horses. Boys cut the long grass and dried it in the sun, and then fed it to the horses. They thrived on it—their coats grew sleek, and their dispositions improved so that some of the men and boys could mount them and actually stay astride as they cantered!

So the Council decided to follow St. Clair's advice further, and a party of seven was selected to make the long trip to St. Louis on horseback.

"It is time you saw something of white men, my son," Chief Pyesa said. "Some chieftains believe they will bring us trouble, but up to now they have been good to us. We have traded with them and lived near them here and there in Canada, with trust on both sides. When you are Chief and Medicine Man of All the Sauk and the Fox, you must know more about our neighbors. I have arranged with White Cloud for you to accompany those who have been chosen."

What a journey it was! Although all eight pretended that the speed of their progress made up for their discomfort, by dusk each Indian slid off his horse and led it. They were a stiff and sorry lot as they tried to resume the loping trot that characterized the Sauk brave. Instead, they limped stiffly along the trail. And the next day brought no relief. That night, after tethering the horses, they gingerly lowered themselves and rested, sighing with relief!

When they were awakened by the rising sun, they resumed their journey on foot. Leaving their camping place, they took turns leading the horses.

So for many days they continued toward the city of St. Louis, resuming their loping run, followed by the trotting horses. After seventeen dawns had awakened them, they came to the end of the dense woods and beheld a sight they had never dreamed of. The forests had been cut down and the earth planted. Whole hillsides were covered with long grass waving and rippling in the sun.

As he looked across the rolling plains and distant rounded hills, Black Hawk felt a sudden sense of shock. The hills looked as if they had been scalped, or like the ugly shaven heads of the Osage tribe; with stumps of murdered trees, like stubble on a shaven head!

A deep anger welled up in him. White men had cut down the strong beautiful trees and changed the countryside into a series of squares and rectangles—the plowed sections looked like buffalo skins; the fields of maize like tanned cowhide; the alfalfa like water where there was none. At last Black Hawk moved to White Cloud's side and spoke.

"Why?" he asked.

"The white man uses wood for everything—for his wickiup, to cook his meals. He does not live out of doors, as his white skin proves, so he needs more wood to burn for warmth."

"The Indian, too, burns wood," Black Hawk protested. "But we eat enough and are warm enough without destroying the forest."

"It's because there are so many of them," White Cloud said.

Anger still smoldering within him, Black Hawk followed White Cloud as the old Peace Chief started down the trail.

"How do they know where they are going?" Black Hawk asked.

"There are no trees for markings. At night when there is no moon, or the stars are hidden, how do they know? The wide trail, with no trees to shade it, is baked hard under the sun. Our feet leave no mark. How can they tell who has passed this way before?"

"There are so many of them," White Cloud said, "they can pass the word along from one to another as fast as a fire travels in a forest."

They ran along the empty road feeling conspicuous. Occasionally, they passed a farm where dogs bayed at them, silhouetted against the whiteness of the road.

Next day they felt they must be nearing the end of the journey, because the farms were much closer together. As they continued, the farms shrank to the size of a Sauk garden—just little squares of planted ground with a wooden house at the back.

"The wickiups are high!" Black Hawk exclaimed. "The white man builds one upon the other."

At one farm where they stopped to ask for water, the frightened farmer walked toward two huge dogs chained to a tree. As the Indians realized what he was about to do, they loped away down the road. And, as he watched the great White Cloud fleeing, like an old scavenging dog driven away from the wickiup, Black Hawk felt the anger grow within him. They could not avenge this indignity because, if they did, their new Spanish father would never grant the request they had come so far to put to him. They had to accept whatever insults were in store for them until that meeting.

When the next sun rose, they saw clouds of smoke in the distance. At first, they thought it signified a forest fire, but then they realized the clouds were too still. It was the smoke of many smudge fires, as if a tribe were grieving. They hurried on. Soon other trails and roads from east to west joined the one they traveled. White men in buckskins with fringes on their jackets passed them going toward the smoke cloud. They knew they were nearing St. Louis.

The little Sauk delegation reluctantly mounted their horses, trying to look proud and impressive as they approached the great city. No one paid any attention to them! They were just another small party traveling toward St. Louis.

Now, from all the roads that ran into the big one, came many other travelers, some walking, some on horseback, and others in wagons. It was the first time Black Hawk had ever seen a wagon. He could hardly take his eyes off the wheels that went round and round, pushing the wagon forward! It seemed such a simple idea! He asked White Cloud why the Sauk never used them or the big, long platforms covered with white skin.

"We have never needed them," White Cloud answered proudly. "White men call them Prairie Ships and use them to travel and carry their belongings. Indian braves and squaws prefer to walk. And the Indian does not worship things because they are his, as white men do. Only the land, the earth under his feet, the trees over his head, are the belongings the Sauk loves. And these cannot be moved from place to place."

There was much truth in what White Cloud said, Black Hawk thought, but he realized how much easier it would be to bring home buffalo and bear meat in a Prairie Ship, pulled by horses, than in slings on the shoulders of four braves!

Then a lighter, flimsier contraption passed them. Black Hawk heard the laughter of the first white woman he had ever seen. Although he had been told what to expect, he was surprised, nevertheless, at the ugly whiteness of her skin and the bright yellow of her hair, and even more surprised by the many colors of her garments, made of some strange fabric he had never seen.

"I don't know what it is," White Cloud answered his question. "It is woven out of much finer thread than anything we know. White men give their squaws many gifts. That is another of the many differences between us. The white man believes in having only one squaw, who is always with him. That is why, when the white man came here from the land of sunrise, he brought his women with him. Foolish!"

Black Hawk thought of Singing Bird and knew if he had her with him, he would want no other squaw. He would like to have her always close so that he could return to her after a sortie or a hunt. His anger against the white man, which had been growing since his first sight of the despoiled forests, softened. But he did not argue with White Cloud.

When the teeth are closed, the tongue does not wag, he thought. Then he forgot even Singing Bird, for they had reached a curve, and there St. Louis stretched before them.

CHAPTER 7

On the outskirts of the city stood a great stockade, which housed not only many scarlet-coated British soldiers but was the largest trading post in America. Here the Indians and white scouts, trappers and hunters brought their skins and furs and were paid either in money or in food, rifles, and ammunition. It was here that St. Clair had sent the Sauk delegation with a letter to Miguel D'Acosta, the Spanish agent.

White Cloud led them through the great gates to the entrance of a long building shaped like the Long House at Saukenuk, but built on a platform, entirely of logs, one laid upon another.

As Black Hawk tethered his horse, he wondered what held the logs in place. While White Cloud took St. Clair's letter from the doeskin pouch, Black Hawk went to examine the logs. He saw that their ends had been hewn so that one fitted into another and kept both in place. As he followed White Cloud and the rest of the party into the building, he wondered why no Sauk or Fox had ever thought of fastening logs firmly together to make a solid, weatherproof wickiup.

White Cloud showed the paper to the guard, who glanced at it and nodded in the direction they were facing. When Black Hawk saw the wood partitions that rose from the floor to the ceiling, he thought, "It's like a beehive full of little cells, each separated from the other."

Outside the office of the Spanish trader another guard stopped them. Again, White Cloud showed St. Clair's letter. The guard took it and, opening the door, disappeared, closing it in their faces. They looked at each other and uttered words of suspicion. Had this man tricked them? Taken their safe-conduct letter from them? But the door reopened, and the tall man signaled them to enter.

Behind a long, highly polished table sat a tall thin man with granite gray hair whom Black Hawk guessed was the Spanish agent, Don Miguel D'Acosta. He was fascinated by the black haircut in the shape of an arrowhead on the man's chin. He had never before seen a beard.

Don Miguel rose and raised his extended arm toward them. "How," he said.

At least that was what it sounded like. The Sauk delegation stopped and looked toward White Cloud.

"It's a greeting," White Cloud explained in their own tongue. (There was no greeting in the Sauk language.)

Black Hawk and the others followed White Chief's example, raising their right arm straight out in front and solemnly said: "How."

D'Acosta beckoned White Cloud to be seated in a strange four-legged contraption next to the table, and their leader complied. The others stood. No one spoke, and the silence remained unbroken until the door opened and the guard ushered in a dark young man with pale skin.

D'Acosta greeted him in Spanish, and the young man addressed himself to White Cloud in the Sauk language.

"I am the interpreter," he said. "I shall explain to you what Don Miguel says to me. My name is Pat-ter-son. I am an American. The guard has gone to fetch more chairs so that you may all sit."

"We need no chairs," Walking Bear said. "We have more faith in the floor, which was meant for sitting."

Patterson repeated this to Don Miguel, who smiled, showing very white teeth, and spoke.

"He bids you sit wherever you will," Patterson said. So they all sat on the floor. Then Patterson asked the Sauk leader to state the reason for their visit. White Cloud told of the capture of Canada by the British, and the English traders' refusal to allow them supplies until the furs and meat were actually brought in by the Sauk hunters. He explained the hardships this would bring to his people and asked that the Spanish father grant them their needs on trust as the French had always done. When Patterson had translated his words, Don Miguel shook his head sadly and replied.

"My friends," Patterson interpreted, "you have come too late. You know the Spanish have always given supplies to all Indians on credit. But now we have been beaten by the French and have lost all rights here."

His listeners moaned softly and swayed their bodies from side to side in grieving before White Cloud spoke.

"Was there great fighting?" the old Peace Chief asked. "With many dead?"

"Yes," D'Acosta answered.

"Is that why the city grieves?" he asked.

"The city does not grieve," D'Acosta answered through the interpreter. "The city celebrates this day. Most whites and many Indians are happy that the French will take over. Perhaps it will work out well for you. There is to be a ceremony in the city square. Come, we shall go together, and after the ceremony, I shall escort you to the French trading headquarters."

"The city celebrates its dead?" Chief White Cloud asked.

"The fighting was not here," Patterson explained, "but far away across the Great Sea. White chiefs agreed to hand over this land to

France."

"Then our treaty is again safe and will be honored," White Cloud said. "We shall be glad to join you in the great dance of celebration."

"It's not a dance," Patterson began. "Come along. You'll see. Don Miguel will provide you with his outriders so that you may attend the ceremony in complete safety. He has asked me to accompany you as a guide."

The Indians murmured their appreciation.

"But Don Miguel asks me to inquire whether you have brought any furs or jewelry with which to pay for food and shelter tonight, for you might not be able to see the French Trade Commissioner before nightfall."

White Cloud signaled to Walking Bear, who quickly left the room.

"We have brought what we thought would be necessary," White Cloud told the interpreter. In a few minutes Walking Bear returned with a rolled buffalo skin. Untying the thong, he unrolled it, displaying moccasins, quirts, a few hides, and some silver and turquoise bracelets.

D'Acosta graciously selected a few pieces of jewelry and a fine, heavy-handed quirt. Taking a large leather pouch from a drawer in the table, he handed White Cloud twenty round pieces of silver from it, which the Peace Chief put into the doeskin pouch. This first glimpse of money did not impress Black Hawk. It was not nearly so pretty as the turquoise-studded bracelets they had traded for it!

But White Cloud seemed pleased, and Patterson said, "This should be more than enough for your return journey."

Then they all went outdoors. D'Acosta and Patterson got into a light wagon, the Indians mounted their horses, clumsily, and followed, while six soldier outriders rode ahead and behind to guard them from violence.

Thus it was that Black Hawk first entered the city called St. Louis. This was something he would think of and talk about for many moons. No one at Saukenuk would believe him when he told of the many buildings and the swarms of men and women afoot and in carriages, all hurrying along.

"The smoke we saw wasn't from funeral fires," Walking Bear said, "but from the many fires inside the wooden wickiups. It must take much wood to warm all these people."

"That is why they cut down the trees that give life to birds and beasts," Black Hawk thought.

The place to which everyone was hurrying was like the great open rectangle at Saukenuk, and was, indeed, the public square. In the center stood a platform, in front of a flagpole about five times higher than the Sauk totem pole.

When D'Acosta's carriage stopped, Patterson stepped down and crossed over to the Sauks.

"Dismount and hold your horses to keep them from rearing," he said. "They may be frightened when the drums begin."

A man was speaking from the platform in Spanish. All around were soldiers in uniform, colonists in buckskins, and ladies dressed in the same beautiful material Black Hawk had noticed on the girl in the wagon on the Great Trail. He could understand nothing the speaker said, so he allowed his attention to wander. He noticed a girl seated in a carriage. Around her shoulders was the most beautiful shawl Black Hawk had ever seen.

A long sharp roll on the drums brought his attention back to the platform.

"They're lowering the Spanish flag and raising the flag of France," Patterson shouted over the noise. Then another speaker came forward and, as the crowd grew quiet, began to address them.

Black Hawk glanced toward the girl in the carriage. How beautiful was the scarf she was wearing! If only he could get it for Singing Bird! He was sure she would like it much more than the scalps Grey Owl flaunted. He *must* have that white scarf, with the red flowers embroidered on it, for her!

Thrusting his horse's lead rope into Walking Bear's hand, he silently made his way to the girl's carriage. She was unaware of him until he touched her arm. Then, seeing him, she screamed. But, as the crowd burst into cheers at that moment, no one heard her except the soldier seated at her side. He sprang to his feet, reaching for his sword.

The girl's face was a white mask of fear, but she was very quick. "Don't Walter," she said to the tall Englishman. "There will be a massacre if you kill him." She forced herself to look into Black Hawk's eyes.

Although the young Sauk warrior did not understand what she said, he saw the fear in her eyes and smiled to show that he meant no harm. But the paint on his face gave his smile the appearance of a fierce grimace. The girl shuddered as Black Hawk touched the scarf, tugging it gently.

"The dirty dog wants your Spanish shawl," the man muttered savagely. "Give it to him, Cora, before I kill him."

As she hesitated, Black Hawk tried to show her he wanted to trade for it. Around his neck was the string of eighteen bear claws, which he had polished to ivory whiteness. Pulling the necklace over his head, he offered it to the girl. She had slipped the scarf from her shoulders and held it toward him at arm's length.

"Take the filthy thing, or he'll be angered," the man advised. She reached out and gingerly took the necklace from Black Hawk. He put the shawl to his cheek, the better to feel its sleek softness. He had bought it! He could take it to Singing Bird!

There was another loud and sudden roll on the drums. All eyes turned toward the platform where the flag of France was being lowered! Black Hawk returned to his party as Patterson explained the surprising events of the last few minutes.

"France, thinking to cement friendship with the colonists, has ceded this country to America," he said.

"Does that mean we will no longer trade with the French?" White Cloud asked.

D'Acosta spoke to Patterson, who translated.

"Don Miguel says, right after the ceremony, he will take you to the Trade Agency of the Americans."

The country had changed hands twice because of the whim of Napoleon in far-off Europe, but of those present at the flag-raising ceremony in St. Louis in 1781, few realized that this was one of the important moments in the life of the new world.

None of the Indians had any idea what was going on, even after D'Acosta had explained the meaning of what they had witnessed. Only when Adams, the American Trade Commissioner, refused their plea for credit did they realize what the change might mean to them.

Disheartened by the thought of their failure, they left the commissioner's office. D'Acosta bade them a sad farewell.

"I wish you well," he said. "I hope that you will not be angered against all whites because of one man's stupidity."

"I can make no promises for my people," White Cloud replied sternly. "Pyesa is War Chief and Medicine Man. I know his anger will be black indeed."

"Take them to the place where they will sleep," D'Acosta said to Patterson, "and try to see that they are not cheated again."

They were escorted to a large building. Patterson spoke to the tavern-keeper, and they were shown to rooms.

"It's time to say goodbye," Patterson said. "I hope when next we meet, the circumstances will be happier."

Knowing that it meant nothing to the Sauks, he did not raise his hand in salute. Instead, he held out his hand. White Cloud took it, and their fingers clasped in a sign of true friendship. Black Hawk liked this white man and felt he was a real friend. But he was too occupied with the beds they were to sleep in to think any more about Patterson.

Not even White Cloud had ever seen a bed! They looked in amazement at these strange objects, and sinking deep into the eiderdown comforter, they laughed as each in turn tried lying on the strange device in the candlelit room.

Then they silently crept down the stairs and out onto the dark veranda, stretched out on the nice hard boards, and slept.

They arose early and were on their way long before sunrise. They wanted to avoid riding, but didn't want to be seen leading their horses out of town. They had been humiliated enough.

CHAPTER 8

The return journey was accomplished in almost complete silence, each Sauk occupied with his own thoughts. White Cloud realized the disastrous consequences of the American's refusal to "stake" them. Without traps or arms, they were wholly dependent on bows and arrows and tomahawks to kill the beasts whose fur and meat they needed, nor could they fight off the marauding Chippewas.

They had enough dried meat to last the winter, but spring would find them without either furs or meat to trade. The maize would not grow before summer. They could not feed their families.

Black Hawk's anger, aroused by his first sight of the ugly stripped hills, surged up again as he thought of the hardships his people would suffer because of the white man's refusal to trust them. But his anger was tempered by an admiration for the white man's skill and knowledge. He thought they had a "medicine" which gave them power over fire. Hadn't he seen a flame which gave light but no heat, coming out of a round, gray stick?

There were a hundred little things he wanted to mull over—the height and size of the buildings, the rigging that raised and lowered the flags, the harness on the horses, the construction of the wagons, and the whole idea of wheels.

In this new mood of wonder he saw things that he had not noticed when they traveled the road before. He paused by a split-rail fence to examine its construction, but soon became interested in the farmer working in the field with a horse-drawn plow. Walking Bear paused beside him.

"What do you stare at, my young friend?" he asked.

"I was just thinking that those furrows are straighter and deeper than those our squaws make," Black Hawk answered. "And the white brave, not his squaw, is behind the plow."

"If we followed that example," Walking Bear said, "we would have no time to train our warriors."

"That is what I was thinking," Black Hawk replied. "A man who takes time to guide the plow cannot be concerned with conquest. Perhaps the white man is not on the warpath. Maybe he is satisfied to feed himself and his squaw and children and will not attack us or threaten Saukenuk."

"What would the squaws do if they had no work?" Walking Bear asked.

"Perhaps they could learn to use the bow and arrow and defend the village when all but the old men and children are out on the hunt or a sortie."

Walking Bear grunted, thinking that too ridiculous to deserve a reply. But Black Hawk knew that one girl, Singing Bird, could shoot better than he could.

The sun was setting when the little party reached a rushing stream and paused to drink and water their horses. As they knelt on the rocky banks, arrows sped past them to plunge into the brook.

Black Hawk, the only warrior in the group, took command. "Lie flat," he cried, and he searched the woods for a target.

"Wa-wa-wa-wa-wehee!"

From all around came the fear-inspiring war cry. But instead of shuddering, Black Hawk stood up, waving his arms. It was the battle cry of the Sauk!

"We are Sauks!" he cried, and returned the battle cry.

Almost immediately, one by one, a shamefaced group of braves emerged from the deep woods.

"What is a war party of Sauk and Fox doing this far from Saukenuk?" Black Hawk asked the leader of the party.

"Runners brought word that the hated Sioux plan an attack on Saukenuk," Sly Fox answered. "Chief Pyesa sent out ten small parties to scout, with orders to attack on sight any band of warriors. We saw your horses, Black Hawk, and—"

"Fortunate for us that your aim was no better," Black Hawk interrupted. "And fortunate for you that we were not Sioux on the warpath!" Then Black Hawk asked about his father.

"He is well, though troubled by this new threat to our village."

"Is there any other news? Are our families well?" Walking Bear asked.

"They are well," Sly Fox said, looking quizzically at Black Hawk. He had been well-named, this tall Sauk chieftain who enjoyed making trouble. And he wanted to get even with Black Hawk for making fun of him in front of his braves. "Your 'brother' Grey Owl has been seen going often to the wickiup of Singing Bird," he added.

White Cloud, overhearing, spoke up. "My sons are with my daughter," he said with simple dignity. "Red Bird and Grey Owl are friends. It is not surprising that Grey Owl should visit our home. He is always welcome."

"I only meant—" Sly Fox began, but White Cloud interrupted him.

"I know what the wily Sly Fox meant," he said, and began climbing back onto the trail. As he passed Black Hawk, he touched the boy's shoulder in friendly sympathy.

"I will ask no more questions," Black Hawk said as he followed White Cloud. "Better hunting!" he called back.

But Sly Fox's words had done their work. Black Hawk was

troubled. He wished the distance between him and Saukenuk would dwindle fast! He touched the Spanish shawl fastened to the thong at his waist, hoping Singing Bird would value it above the scalps on Grey Owl's spear.

When at last they reached the cliffs overlooking their village, they saw a strange sight. A stockade, like the one at St. Louis, had been built around the entire village. Long poles had been driven into the ground and fastened together with dried buffalo intestines, so they formed a high fence. At each end was a great gate.

"The threat to Saukenuk must be serious," White Cloud said. They urged their tired bodies to greater speed.

Even before they reached the stockade, the gates swung back noiselessly, for the sentinels had recognized the White Cloud party. Black Hawk broke into a run, for he had seen that Red Bird was one of the sentinels.

"How's Father?" Black Hawk asked.

"He's well, and will be glad to know of your safe return."

"And Singing Bird?" Black Hawk asked, trying to sound casual and evidently not succeeding, because Red Bird's black eyes twinkled.

"She's well, too."

"What of my brother, Grey Owl?"

"He seems very happy. I don't think he missed you at all."

Belatedly, Black Hawk remembered he was a brave with a position to uphold. "Send the other guard to notify Chief Pyesa that Chief White Cloud and his party have returned safely," he said, hoping White Cloud would think that was why he had run ahead.

Red Bird smiled knowingly and ordered the other guard to awaken Chief Pyesa and inform him that Chief White Cloud would await his orders in the Council House.

The others hurried to their families, but Black Hawk lingered on.

"Red Bird," he asked, "do you know where Grey Owl is now?"

"He has spent many nights sitting in front of our fire," Red Bird answered.

"So I have heard," Black Hawk muttered angrily.

"But so have I, my friend," Red Bird said, smiling. "I cannot remember ever spending so many evenings sitting there."

Black Hawk waited to hear no more, but ran toward White Cloud's wickiup, where Singing Bird slept in her own tipi. He must find out once and for all if Singing Bird favored Grey Owl above himself. Life would be very bleak without her, but he had to know the truth. With her father away and Red Bird guarding the gate, Grey Owl had a wonderful opportunity to be alone with Singing Bird. He might even be proposing to her!

It was the custom among his tribe to set fire to a small birch twig when a man wished to marry a girl. With this little torch, he visited her in her tipi in the dead of night. If she were asleep, he wakened her by waving the lighted torch before her eyes, but he was not allowed either to touch or speak to her.

If the girl wished to reject her suitor, she turned her back on him. But if she wished to accept him, she blew out the little flame.

As Black Hawk neared the group of tipis that housed White Cloud's family, his worst fears were confirmed. On the ground near the wickiups were white birch shavings and a small charred piece of birch twig. He went quietly toward the tipi in which Singing Bird slept. It was dark! There was no sign of a flaming torch. Grey Owl had been there and had been rejected or had not yet come. Black Hawk raced back to the little pile of shavings and began whirling the still warm branch twig in them, frantically breathing a prayer to the Great Spirit to ignite the twig. Finally, it flickered and caught fire. He sighed gratefully and hurried to Singing Bird's tipi.

Softly he raised the buffalo-hide flap and entered, holding aloft his tiny torch. Singing Bird was asleep, and again he breathed a sigh of relief.

He knelt and moved the flame toward her. She turned. Her eyes opened, and she saw him without the least surprise. It was almost as if she had been expecting him, even dreaming of his coming, and waking was but the continuation of the dream.

Without hesitating, she blew out the torch.

Black Hawk remained crouched before her, too exalted to move. He felt that everything he had ever wanted had been granted him. How he longed to touch Singing Bird! But this he must not do. After a long moment, he went out of the tipi into the moonlit night.

For some time he walked aimlessly within the great new fence. At last he heard footsteps, and presently he recognized Grey Owl. Poor Grey Owl! Of course, he would be out walking in grief. Black Hawk could afford to be generous now. And in his mood of overwhelming joy, he had no wish for anyone else to suffer. He was glad he could meet his defeated rival alone and in the darkness.

"Grey Owl," he called softly.

So deeply was Grey Owl immersed in his own thoughts, he was completely unaware of Black Hawk's nearness.

"Who's there?" Then he recognized Black Hawk.

"Black Hawk!" he cried, running forward. "Brother!" He threw his arms around Black Hawk. "I've been walking as if on air for hours."

"I don't understand. Do you mean *you* are happy?"

"When should a man be happier than when the girl he has chosen for his wife blows out the torch?"

"But she didn't," Black Hawk said. "She couldn't have!"

"Why not?" Grey Owl demanded heatedly. "Am I, then, so

hideous to look upon? Why shouldn't Crescent Moon accept me as a husband?"

"Crescent Moon!" Black Hawk's mouth opened in amazement. Then everything became clear to him. "Crescent Moon!" he shouted, hugging Grey Owl. "There's no reason why she shouldn't welcome you as her husband. You are handsome and brave. You have eleven scalps on your spear!"

"I was afraid you might be angry," Grey Owl said.

"Angry? Why should I be?"

"Because I take Singing Bird's handmaiden from her."

"She will need no companion now," Black Hawk said jubilantly, "other than myself."

"Black Hawk, you mean you've actually had the courage after all this time..."

"What do you mean—courage? I've never lacked courage for anything."

"No? Then what were you waiting for? Why, Singing Bird had almost given up on you! She tried everything—even flirting with me—to make you jealous. Nothing happened."

"Grey Owl, I've been a fool!"

The two young braves looked at each other in understanding and affection. Linking arms, they resumed their walk. There was much to be discussed. Crescent Moon had not been adopted into the Sauk tribe. Would Pyesa allow his adopted son to marry an outsider?

"I'll do my best to persuade him," Black Hawk promised.

"Thank you," Grey Owl said. "You know that my life is yours always, for it was you who spared it when you could have killed me. Crescent Moon, too, feels that she owes her life to you, and therefore has a double loyalty since she would always be loyal to me."

"I'm sure Father will understand," Black Hawk said. "Let us talk of other things. I want to know about the threat of a Sioux attack and the likelihood of war."

"And I want to know all that happened in St. Louis."

They paced around the great wall, unaware of the passing of time. Suddenly they noticed the sky was streaked with pink. Guiltily, they sneaked back toward their tipi, and in minutes both were asleep.

CHAPTER 9

Pyesa was delighted at the thought of the wedding of his son with the daughter of his old friend. He readily consented to a double ceremony so Grey Owl and Crescent Moon could be married at the same time.

What a ceremony it was! All thought of a Sioux attack was forgotten. The entire village, including the Fox section of Saukenuk, across the tiny river and now outside the stockade, was invited to participate.

Fish were caught to be baked on heated stones. Dried buffalo meat was soaked in the salty brine made of water and the skin of the wild hog. Young girls braided shafts of wheat and maize into their hair and hammered silver bracelets to wear.

Pyesa and Black Hawk were pleased and flattered by the various preparations for the festivities.

Pyesa summoned Black Hawk for a talk. "My son," he began seriously, "now that you are a man, you must prepare to take on your shoulders the responsibilities that will be yours as son of the Chief and Medicine Man of the Sauk and the Fox."

"I want you to be proud of me, Father," Black Hawk replied.

"Perhaps you are old enough now to understand the need for cruelty," Pyesa continued. He turned away as though he were gazing into the far-distant past.

"It was long before you were born that the white men first came," he went on. "Before that, there was little fighting between Indian tribes. Some had their own villages; others roamed the woods or plains, sleeping wherever they found themselves at sunset. There were enough fish in the waters, birds in the air, and beasts in the forests to give plenty of food for all."

"White men, too, seek food," Black Hawk said. "And there are so many of them."

"They are without number," Pyesa sighed. "They come from Canada, from far-distant parts of this country, from across the Great Sea."

"Where will they stop?" Black Hawk asked.

"They will not stop," Pyesa answered. "They will go everywhere, trampling beneath the wheels of their Prairie Ships not only the beasts but all who live in the forests. It is not just hunger that drives them. If it were, they would stop where there is enough to eat."

"What is it, then?"

"It is something we do not have, so it is hard for me to name it. St. Clair tried to make us understand, but it is not easy. Just as there are differences between the Sauk and the Sioux, the Osage and the Algonquin, so there are differences between the white tribes—the Spanish, the French, the English, and now the Americans, who used to be English. The white man wants more than food," Pyesa went on.

"So does the Sauk brave."

"But the Sauk does not care to own the land he lives on."

"We care about Saukenuk. It is ours."

"I *said* it was difficult to put into words," Pyesa sighed again, "for I am a War Chief, not a speaker. But we never used to think Saukenuk was ours any more than we thought the sky was ours, or the forests or lakes or rivers. Then the white man came and wanted the land where Saukenuk now stands."

"I didn't know that!"

"It was long ago. They offered only beads at first, and later whiskey and other things we did not need. Their insistence taught us to think that this village and all the country given to us by the

French belongs to us. So now we stand in the way of the white man. He would like to build a great trail running through where Saukenuk now stands. And because we will not give up our homes and our hunting grounds, they refuse to lend us rifles and ammunition."

"So that is why!" Black Hawk exclaimed.

"Yes. And that, too, is the reason for the Sioux attacks. The whites supplied them with rifles. It is thought that part of the terms of the agreement was that they attack the Sauk and Fox. The whites are not satisfied to outnumber us. They turn Indian against Indian. And so, we must do what we can to make up for this. We must frighten them by painting our faces and our bodies. We must scalp. We must maim and mutilate so that white man and Indian alike are frightened even by a few of us."

Black Hawk was silent.

"Now that you are to marry and will have sons of your own," the chief continued, "you will know you must do everything to frighten off anyone who threatens your family and your home. The only way to keep Saukenuk safe is by making our enemies believe we are fiercer and stronger than they are. So we must make many sorties. We must seek out trouble before it can find us."

"I will do my best to make Singing Bird and Saukenuk safe forever," Black Hawk said.

Pyesa looked with pride upon his son.

"You will one day be Chief and Medicine Man of All the Sauk and Fox," he said. His eyes twinkled suddenly. "Has not Watanka, the Great Spirit, proclaimed you the great leader?"

Black Hawk smiled back at him. "Who knows what the Great Spirit wants? But that fortune has smiled upon me I do know, for have I not a loyal brother and fine friends? And have I not the finest wife in all Saukenuk?"

"Not yet," Pyesa answered. "But you will after the ceremony."

Black Hawk was much impressed by the great double ceremony. The sound of two hundred drums was enough to send shivers down his long, straight back! A hundred gaily bedecked girls and feathered braves took part in the exciting Dance of Fertility. Pyesa and White Cloud—two great and beloved chiefs—stood on the ceremonial rock in front of the tall totem pole and asked Watanka for the happiness of these four young people and that their sons would bring pride to the Sauk nation. The great bonfire—the fire of life—made pictures that would stay with Black Hawk all his life.

He was still in a haze of happiness two days later when he, with Grey Owl and Red Bird as lieutenants, led his party of eighty warriors on a dangerous mission into the distant Sioux country across the Father of Waters to the north and east of Saukenuk.

Twenty-one times the sun rose on the Indian village before there was word of him or his men. At last the entire party returned. Not one man had been lost! Praises were sung of Black Hawk's leadership. It seemed true indeed that the Great Spirit smiled upon this young warrior and all who followed him. He had led his party to the Sioux hunting ground, where the warriors were engaged in the buffalo hunt. The Sioux were caught off guard, and forty-two were killed by Black Hawk's party. Thirty-five scalps graced their spears. And not a Sauk lost! This was a tale that would be told in dances for many nights to come. But Pyesa was not pleased, for Black Hawk's spear flaunted no scalp.

"I couldn't, Father," Black Hawk confessed. "I tried. But they were not molesting us. They were killing their own buffalo on their own hunting grounds to satisfy the hunger of their own families."

"Were their squaws with them?"

"Yes. Some carried papooses."

"Were any killed?"

Black Hawk forced himself to face the anger in his father's voice. "No."

"No children?"

"No."

"And none were scalped?"

"No, Father. They were huddled together, not joining in the fight. They did not even threaten us. I thought to massacre them would serve to bring on an attempt at reprisal."

Pyesa's eyes smoldered. Such anger shook him that for a moment it seemed as if he might strike his son. Then, controlling his rage, he forced himself to speak quietly.

"Do you kill the doe in the springtime?"

"No," Black Hawk answered, puzzled.

"Or the fawns? Or the cow buffalo or the calves?"

"No."

"Why not?" Pyesa asked.

"Because the breed would die out if the females and their young were killed," Black Hawk replied.

"But do you feel the same way toward the fox, the wolf, or any other beast that is not meant for eating, but steals our food and attacks us? You want those breeds to increase, too?"

"*That* is why we are to kill squaws and papoose? To kill off the breed? But that's horrible! It's—"

"Hear now, O stubborn son of mine," Pyesa interrupted. "A party of Sioux broke through the guard at the stream where you and White Cloud stopped to water the horses."

"No!" Black Hawk exclaimed. "Did they get through to Saukenuk? I knew Sly Fox was not the one to be entrusted with such a mission."

"Sly Fox returned to us," Pyesa said gravely.

"What did he say?"

"He said nothing, for his tongue had been removed." Pyesa spoke cruelly, for he wanted to shock Black Hawk into a realization of their danger. "He was left at the gate at night. In the morning we found him, dying. There were no other survivors. Had you fought as Sauk warriors are trained to fight, the Sioux would have thought we were seeking reprisal. They might have been frightened off and never attacked us again. Now that we have been soft with them, we must send parties out at every point where they might break through. We shall have to be constantly on the alert. It may cost many lives."

Black Hawk said nothing, but in his heart he knew that even had he known of the mutilation of Sly Fox, he still would not have felt like ruthlessly killing women and babies. This troubled him, for he wanted to please Pyesa.

He could not understand why he felt that needless killing was wrong. It would be so much easier to agree with his father. There was no one with whom he could talk it over. He knew that even Singing Bird, his wife, who was so close to him in many ways, would not understand. She had been brought up to believe as Pyesa did. She would raise fine sons who would enjoy killing and scalping and bloody fighting.

Not long afterward a runner, nearly exhausted from days and nights of steady travel, came bearing terrifying news. The guards at the gate half carried him to Pyesa.

"Soaring Eagle!" the chief exclaimed. "What brings you home? You were with Black Bear on the sortie far to the Northland."

"We captured a scouting party of Sioux," the messenger gasped. "One begged for mercy and said if we spared his life, he'd tell us—" He choked, and one of the Council held a goatskin water bag to the runner's parched lips. Soaring Eagle gulped the water, then continued:

"He told us the party that killed Sly Fox at the stream got through to the plains below and brought messages to the Osage. They will attack Saukenuk in great numbers, not from the forest but from the lowlands."

The listeners gasped. No one had ever thought of the possibility of attack from the valley. Pyesa sat in silence for several moments, then he spoke.

"You have served your people well, Soaring Eagle. Moments are precious, and you have sped on winged feet. There is still time to prepare."

He took a gourd filled with bear grease and handed it to his guard who still supported the weary messenger.

"Take him to his tipi," he ordered. "Have the squaws rub his tired body with this medicine."

The news traveled fast from tipi to tipi, and squaws and braves gathered in little groups to discuss this threat to their very existence. They assembled in the square, looking anxiously toward the Long House where Pyesa sat in lonely Council.

Black Hawk and Singing Bird were in the anxiously awaiting crowd. Eyes were turned toward Black Hawk. For was he not to be their future leader? Was he not the leader whom Watanka smiled upon?

At last Pyesa lifted the flap of the Long House and stepped into the clearing.

"Watanka, the Great Spirit, has spoken to me," he announced. "We are to go forth to meet the Osage warriors at a place called Ashawequa. There we shall wipe them out, though they be as many as needles of a fir tree."

A murmur rustled through the crowd. Watanka had spoken to their chief. If they followed him, they would be safe.

"Black Hawk will lead the warriors," Pyesa said. Suddenly to the young brave the world seemed very wonderful, for the crowd roared approval. He had again been chosen by Watanka to lead them. Singing Bird touched his arm, and he smiled down at her. Then he turned and made his way through the crowd to his father's side. The shouts grew louder, and Pyesa held his arm high for silence.

"Our sorties have taken many of our best fighters from Saukenuk," Pyesa said. "We shall need every warrior here to go with Black Hawk. But Red Bird, I leave you in charge of the defense of Saukenuk."

There was a murmur of surprise.

"I need to leave a brave warrior," Pyesa explained. "One who can train the old men and the squaws to defend you, should we not succeed. For I, too, shall be gone. I go to Ashawequa with Black Hawk."

Chief Pyesa serving under Black Hawk! This was unheard of!

"I go," he said, "lest the Osage surrender and wish to treaty with us. Treaties may be signed only by the Chief and Medicine Man. If they surrender, it may be possible to gain not only freedom from attack by the Osage and Sioux, but an agreement with the whites. We shall leave the sunrise after the next sunrise. Meanwhile, there is much to be done. Red Bird, Black Hawk, Grey Owl, Walking Bear, and my Council will meet with me here now. The squaws and maidens will begin gathering swamp grass from the riverbank. Bring it in bundles to the totem. Then, braid it into ropes, three strands to a rope, sixty paces long. Start now, for the ropes must be finished before we leave."

He raised his hand as a silent blessing and reentered the Long House. Black Hawk followed him. Once inside, Pyesa grasped his son's arm almost fiercely.

"There are things I must say to you before the others come. I am going on this sortie because of you. You must learn how the Sauk warrior fights. You must watch me and follow my example. You must be taught to harden yourself for the good of our people, for I want you to be Chief and Medicine Man of All the Sauk and the Fox when I am gone to the Happy Hunting Grounds. But I do not want our people to have a weak-stomached squaw as their leader. Whether this is my wish or the will of Watanka, I know not. But I know it is *my* wish."

"Then it is the wish of the Great Spirit," Black Hawk said. His father looked deep into the unwavering eyes of his son and nodded. "Perhaps it is," he said.

CHAPTER 10

When the Council and the warriors had assembled, Pyesa drew a map on the hard dirt floor with an arrow.

"The Osage, like the Sioux, are horsemen," he said. "In the woods a foot soldier has the advantage. If we awaited them here behind our stockade, they could fling lighted torches and shoot flaming arrows faster than we could kill them. Then we would have two enemies to fight at once—the Osage and fire. Saukenuk might be destroyed. There is a long level field covered with short grass that extends from the Osage country toward Saukenuk. That is the way they must come. But at Ashawequa there are two small rises, overgrown with blackberry bushes and vine of the white grape. Only waist high, they afford no cover for a man on horseback, but many of us can stand crouched behind them unseen. Soaring Eagle will take a half less twenty of our braves and hide in the copse on one rise. Black Hawk will take a half less twenty and hide in readiness in the vineyard. I, with forty braves, will be stationed here."

He settled the tip of his arrow at a point equidistant from the circles he had drawn, but behind them, toward Saukenuk.

"They'll ride you down, Chief Pyesa!"

"Let one of us take the center position!"

"Forty men have no chance against a crowd of wild horsemen!"

Pyesa raised his hand for silence. "We will be the bait to lure the wolves into the trap. Not many will reach us, for between the two hillocks will be stretched the swamp-grass ropes the women are braiding. Two men will be at each end of every rope. As the horde of horsemen near me and my forty braves, the rope holders will pull them taut at the height of an arrow."

Black Hawk could discern his father's purpose in this strategy. "The ropes will hit the horses halfway between the hoof and knee," he said. "They will stumble and fall."

His father looked at him approvingly. "That is the plan. They will fall over each other, the ones behind falling over those at the forefront of the charge. Those who are thrown can be attacked by my small party, for they will be at a disadvantage. The horsemen who follow will find they cannot pass the blockade and will veer to both sides, where Black Hawk and Soaring Eagle will be waiting for them. In the low underbrush, their horses will be useless. They will have to dismount and fight on equal terms!"

When the warriors understood their chief's plans, they looked at him with awe.

"The Great Spirit must indeed be with us to give us such a leader," someone called.

"I could never have conceived the plan without Watanka's help," Pyesa said humbly.

The next dawn saw the gathering in the Great Square of every brave able to fight. Red Bird, with Walking Bear serving under him, was to assign every squaw, maiden, and old man to parts of the stockade wall, where they would remain on guard.

The long ropes of swamp grass were coiled and tied to a horse's back. The sky had begun to lighten in the east as the great force of nearly four hundred braves left Saukenuk. Pyesa led the way. Black Hawk, just behind the chief, was side by side with Soaring Eagle.

"I've been wondering whether the Sioux informer whose life was spared might have told other Sioux that he had given us information in exchange for his life," said Black Hawk.

"A warrior who would betray his people could not be trusted to be loyal to his enemies," Soaring Eagle replied. "This scalp is proof that he will tell no more tales." He held it up for Black Hawk to see.

"He was an ugly fellow with dirty hair." He smiled at Black Hawk's disgust.

When they paused at nightfall, Black Hawk threw himself down beside his father. As they relaxed before the fire, Black Hawk asked the Chief what part the Great Spirit had played in the working out of such an unusual plan of attack. For no one had ever before thought of erecting a barricade against a cavalry charge.

"You *do* believe the plan was given you by the Great Spirit?" Black Hawk asked.

"What a man believes should be locked behind his teeth," Pyesa admonished.

"Surely you must believe that some power brought you a picture of the very place where we should wait! How would you have known of the two hillocks and the name Ashawequa?"

"The Great Spirit may have put the thought in my mind," Pyesa agreed reluctantly. "Certainly it is well that all who take part in the fight believe so."

"But how else could you have pictured the exact spot—"

"It *might* have been because in my boyhood I hunted grouse and pheasant in those little copses."

Father and son exchanged a companionable smile.

"Someday you will *have* to tell me what you really believe, Father. I've seen you take remedies from the otterskin medicine bag—remedies which brought relief. Are they remedies of the body, or are they 'medicine' of the spirit?"

"Whatever you make of them, they are," Pyesa stated flatly, and would say no more.

At last they arrived at a spot that exactly fitted Pyesa's description of Ashawequa. Needing no further instructions, Black Hawk led his braves toward the south hillock, and Soaring Eagle took his warriors to the underbrush-covered high ground to the northward.

The swamp grass ropes were unpacked and brought to Pyesa. Four men were ordered to place one rope nearly two hundred paces from where they stood. They laid it flat in the long field grass, running across the width of the little valley. Standing upon a rock, Pyesa's eyes searched the lane for any sign of the rope. Satisfied that it was invisible to the unknowing eye, he had another rope laid, in like fashion, across the valley's width, some hundred paces nearer. And the third rope was then placed fifty paces from where he stood.

Then he explained to the warriors what they were to do.

All night they waited and all the next morning, keeping constantly on guard. The men wondered if the informer had lied and the Sioux party had never reached the Osage. Just as they were about to question the wisdom of their chief, one of the sentinels cried out, and the braves, rising to their feet, saw a great cloud of dust on the distant plains. The Osage were on the warpath!

"Let us hope they get here before the sun goes down," Pyesa said. "For then its rays will slant in their eyes and blind them to the presence of the rope as well as of our men."

He walked from one group to another, encouraging the warriors, reassuring himself that his orders were understood. Last of all he spoke to Black Hawk.

"My son, much depends on you. The Osages must not get through to Saukenuk. If for any reason the horsemen ride us down and go on, follow them without delay. But try to stop them here, and believe that the Great Spirit will give strength to the ropes."

Then he returned to his men, whom he ordered to kneel with bowstrings drawn as a challenge to the oncoming enemy. He himself, in his Chief's headdress and full regalia of Medicine Man, stood fearlessly in front of them.

The dust cloud drew nearer! Suddenly came the horrifying war cry of the Osage! They had seen Pyesa and his men, and the air echoed with a sound like the screeching of a thousand wounded wildcats. They came on, twirling knives and tomahawks above their shaven heads, the bloodlust gleaming in their sun-dazzled eyes.

The first solid wall of horses and screaming savages passed the first rope and the second. Still Pyesa and his men held their ground! Then Pyesa shouted, and the third rope sprang out of the grass like a great snake, striking the horses' legs. Pyesa's men fired as the animals fell. Then came the second rope. More horses plunged and reared, throwing their riders. The loud neighs of the injured horses joined the hideous cries of the warriors. When those in the rear tried to come to the aid of their fallen brothers, the first rope came into action.

Black Hawk, waiting until the enemy should divide and come toward him, saw three Osage warriors break through the mass of bodies and drive their horses straight toward Pyesa. If he fired, he would disclose the location of his hidden braves. But he could not let them kill his father!

He saw one of the Osage fall from his horse, an arrow protruding from his chest. Then Black Hawk was running, hurdling the prone bodies of his companions, crouching as he ran so that no one could see from which direction he had come. As he emerged into the little clearing, he saw an Osage plunge a spear into his father's side before the Osage was struck down by one of Pyesa's braves. As Pyesa fell, Black Hawk saw an Osage slide from his horse and bend over the chief. The last rays of the dying sun gleamed on a raised scalping knife held aloft by an arm encircled by blue and yellow bracelets.

Then Black Hawk was in the thick of it. In a fury, he struck fiercely, slashing the wrist that held the knife, then plunging his own knife into the Osage warrior's neck. Other Osages surged forward. Straddling his father's prone body, Black Hawk held them off with vicious blows of tomahawk and knife.

Then, as if from the dead, a voice spoke to him.

"Black Hawk," Pyesa said. "Go to your post. They must not be allowed to get through. Forget me. Your place is with your men."

Black Hawk signaled to two of Pyesa's braves to guard their fallen chief, then ran back toward the hill. The enemy was dispersing to north and south, but he led his men against the approaching horsemen, pulling the surprised warriors from their mounts. Again and again his tomahawk rose and fell. Again and again his knife flashed in the growing darkness.

The Sauk braves, inspired by Black Hawk's ferocity, fought desperately. Under the fury of their merciless attack, the Osage warriors, unused to foot fighting, fought the brambles and heavy underbrush as hard as they fought their human enemies. Finally, they turned and tried to flee, but Black Hawk followed and cut them down. Only when rout was assured did he remember his father. Rage coursed through his veins like a slow flame, and he felt the need for bloody revenge.

Wiping his blood-clotted knife on his thigh, he bent down to collect his first scalp. Once he had done it, the second was easier, and the third gave him no pause at all. Stooping and rising, he made his way back toward his father. At first he could not see him, for he was covered with a pile of bodies. They were Sauk warriors who had died protecting their chief.

Reverently, Black Hawk pulled them from the grim pile, hoping that their deaths had not been in vain, that his father had not been scalped. At the very bottom of the pile was Pyesa, unscalped and still breathing!

He jerked the spear from Pyesa's side, stopping the spouting blood flow with scooped up dirt. Presently, Pyesa recognized his son.

"Did any break through toward Saukenuk?" he asked weakly.

"Not one," Black Hawk said.

"Have any escaped?"

"They are trying to. Our braves are following them."

"You should be leading them," Pyesa said. It was then Black Hawk dropped the mass of tangled scalps at his father's side in the blood-soaked dust.

"These are to avenge you, Father," he said. "Lie still now. I will come back quickly." He left to rejoin his men but saw at once that he was no longer needed. Soaring Eagle's braves and his own men were sending a mass of arrows after the desperately fleeing Osage warriors. The ground was like a field of maize after a tornado. Everywhere were sprawled lifeless bodies.

"Take care of our wounded braves," Black Hawk ordered, as he saw the last Osage fall with an arrow in his back. Stooping, he pulled up one of the swamp-grass ropes, approached a horse, and threw the rope around its neck like a halter. After catching another horse, he tethered the two animals and returned to his father. Under Pyesa's gaze, he mutilated two bodies of the dead Osage, carried them to the horses, and lashed them firmly on their backs. Then he whipped the horses across their rumps and sent them off, carrying their gruesome message to the Osage. They broke into a gallop and headed in the direction from which they had come.

When Black Hawk returned to Pyesa, his father looked at him with eyes that were both sad and proud.

"You have learned to fight as an Indian fights," he said, in a tone almost of regret. "It had to be, even though something of your spirit has been lost." He struggled to sit up. "You will be Chief of All the Sauk and the Fox. The Council cannot deny you after this great coup."

"No!" Black Hawk shouted. "You will get well. This is but a flesh wound…" He did not continue, for his father was looking at him with the well-loved smiling eyes that seemed to chide him for being foolish.

"I am dying," he said. "I want you to promise that you will never let the Sauk be driven from Saukenuk by red men or white. Promise!"

"I promise," Black Hawk whispered huskily. Pyesa smiled and lay back on the ground, satisfied and at peace.

As the young brave knelt beside him, Pyesa reached beneath his own body and painfully brought forth a soiled and bloody object. It was the otterskin pouch—symbol of the Medicine Man.

"It is yours now, Black Hawk."

"You never did tell me its secret."

Pyesa's eyes crinkled at the corners. "Its secret lies here," he said, tapping his brow. "And here." He touched his heart. "Medicine is only good if you believe in it. Whatever you wish to believe you can make the truth." He closed his eyes, taking the secret of the pouch with him to the Happy Hunting Ground.

Others could lift the body of their chief to the back of a horse and ride with it on the long trail to Saukenuk. Black Hawk had done everything his father had hoped for and, in so doing, had honored him in the only way he wanted to be honored.

He looked down at the bloody mass of scalps at his feet, and from them to the corpse-strewn field. The exhilaration of the fight, the spur of his rage, had left him feeling only disgust and horror. He was suddenly filled with deep grief and a sense of loss, not only for his father, but for something vague that he could not explain even to himself.

CHAPTER 11

Before the returning warriors reached the Little Woods outside Saukenuk, Black Hawk unlashed Pyesa's body from the horse and lowered it gently to the ground. After cleansing it and repairing the war paint, he ordered six braves to carry it on their shoulders, knowing his father would not have wanted to return home on horseback. All the braves took up the mournful chant of the death dirge. Red Bird, on guard on the walls of the stockade, heard them from afar off. Soon all Saukenuk knew of the disaster.

That night smudge fires were lighted, and the body of Pyesa was placed on a platform below the totem pole, where his spirit could watch the dances portraying the events of his life and of his gallant death.

It was dawn before Black Hawk left the Great Square and sought the solitude of his own wickiup. Singing Bird met him, putting her hand on his arm in gentle sympathy. But he could not shake off the mood of self-disgust which choked him, even making him forget his grief. He stalked past her toward the tipi, then turned and smiled at her bitterly.

"My spear is now adorned with more scalps than Grey Owl's. Do you like me any better?"

"Oh, my husband," she cried, "I like you as you are. Gentle and strong."

"No longer gentle," he said.

Next morning, he was summoned to the Long House, where he was told the Council deemed it the will of Watanka that he become

Head Chief and Medicine Man of the Sauk and the Fox tribes. When he had formally accepted and been handed the otterskin bag as a symbol of his power, the Council remained to discuss matters of government of Saukenuk.

Black Hawk soon discovered that there was much to learn about his people as well as their government. He soon found that many of the Fox, across the Rock River, felt they had been shut out when Pyesa's stockade was not built around their part of the village.

Actually, the building of the stockade should not have been the concern of either Pyesa or of Black Hawk. It was the duty of the Peace Chief to see to the future safety of the village. So Black Hawk could have avoided all responsibility and added the burden to the shoulders of aging White Cloud, but he believed that the Fox had a just grievance and that anything that divided his people must be corrected.

Until the building of the stockade, Saukenuk had been one village with the river running through the center. Black Hawk was determined that it should again be united. White Cloud gave his permission to order the young Sauks and Foxes alike to bring in dead trees and build a stockade around the part of the village that stood on the opposite shore.

With the Osage and the Sioux abandoning hostilities, Black Hawk believed there was no longer need for so many bands of warriors in the field. He sent runners to call in the fighting braves. Upon their return they were put to work on the new stockade.

Only the Chippewas remained troublesome, still trespassing on Sauk hunting grounds. They must be taught a lesson. So Black Hawk ordered Red Bird to take charge of a sortie against them.

Then he set the squaws and every brave, who was not out with Red Bird, to work constructing a bridge-like floor suspended from stockade to stockade across the river. It was a colossal job. But when completed, and men, women, and children had crossed over it safely, Saukenuk was again one village.

Somehow this work gave Black Hawk almost as big a thrill as he had felt when fighting to avenge Pyesa, but it was a warmer, happier feeling. For the hundredth time, he wondered whether in his life there would be an end to fighting. He wanted for his people a peaceful existence in this friendly village.

Although the Chippewas were a nuisance, they were marauders rather than attackers. It seemed to Black Hawk that his village would be safe. There remained only two possible threats—hunger, brought on by the ever-growing scarcity of buffalo and game, and the whites.

When Red Bird returned, he brought more than the good news of a victory over the Chippewas; he brought back the buffalo meat and many pelts. If the furs could be traded in St. Louis for flour, rice, and other staples, there would be no need to fear hunger for the coming year.

The meat was packed in baskets of woven swamp grass and put in the shallow water of Rock River, where it would keep fresh. Instead of sending braves to St. Louis with the heavy furs, Black Hawk had the pelts dried, tanned, and stretched. Then he sent runners to Francis St. Clair, the only white man who had ever set foot in Saukenuk.

The runners returned with the information that the old trader was now living at a little lake some distance to the north—Lac St. Clair, named in his honor, where one of the runners had gone to find him.

The maize was shoulder high before St. Clair answered Black Hawk's message by appearing one day at the village. He asked for an audience with White Cloud, whom he knew. Having seen the messenger hurrying toward the Long House, Black Hawk came quickly.

"Stop!" he ordered. "There is another white with him," he

explained to White Cloud. "I promised Pyesa that no white but St. Clair would set foot within the stockade."

"A friend of the French trader is a friend of the Sauks," White Cloud objected. "To offend his friend is to offend him."

"Then we shall both go and meet them outside the gates," Black Hawk answered. "We can have the skins stretched on poles on the river's shore below the village and discuss the trade there."

Outside the closed gate, the two white men grew restless.

"Thought you said they were friendly Indians, Frank," the stranger said.

"I do not understand," St. Clair replied. "Never before have they kept me outside the gate. Perhaps this Black Hawk is not a friend."

With suspicion on both sides, conditions were not favorable for a friendly meeting. But when the gates swung open and the two chiefs appeared, Black Hawk and the stranger liked each other at once.

St. Clair knew better than to raise his hand in what most whites mistakenly thought was the correct formal address. Instead, he stepped forward with hand outstretched. He and White Cloud clasped hands.

"This is the Chief of the Sauk and the Fox—Black Hawk," White Cloud said in Sauk.

"Welcome," Black Hawk said, speaking the only tongue he knew, and held out his hand.

There is no word in the Sauk language for "friend." St. Clair hesitated, then said, "This is George Davenport, the trader."

As he turned with hand outstretched, Black Hawk looked into the deep-set, kindly eyes of a young man. Davenport saw a tall, slender, muscular Indian, with a long, thin nose and eyes in which he detected great loneliness. As the two men shook hands, each felt their meeting important. When Davenport spoke in Sauk, Black Hawk felt he had at last met someone to whom he could talk.

"The good George has been studying with young Patterson," St. Clair explained. "He now speaks the language of the Sauk better than I."

"Come," Black Hawk said, leading the way. "We shall go to the riverbank where you can see the hides we are tanning. Later we can talk. The boys will catch the leaping trout and bake them on heated stones. We will fill our bellies while our mouths are full of words."

As they walked through an apple orchard toward the river, St. Clair explained that Davenport, an American, had taken over much of the trading in this part of the country.

Both men exclaimed over the beauty and quality of the skins. Then Black Hawk, seating himself on the pine needles, invited them to take their places on a flat rock nearby.

"M'sieur Davenport would like to open a trading post within your great village," St. Clair explained. "He believes many white traders can be brought here and that they will give much silver for the furs and meat the Sauk braves bring in."

"We have no use for silver," White Cloud answered. Davenport gave a friendly laugh. Black Hawk liked the sound of it.

"Only the white man loves money, Frank," he chuckled.

"The white man uses it to trade for the things *he* needs," St. Clair continued. "Why not save a step and learn to use it as he does?"

"It is simpler to trade what one does not need for what one wants," Black Hawk answered.

"And what is it your people want?" Davenport asked.

"Only the things that make food," the chieftain explained. "We can kill more animals than we need to eat—as long as our hunting grounds are left unmolested. We can grow maize and corn enough to make bread to mix with dried meat for pemmican. We want nothing except the long-barreled carbines to shoot buffalo and bear."

"I will give you those," Davenport said quickly.

"Without our paying first with money that we do not have?"

"Without any payment. When you trade me your furs, I will take off the cost of the rifles and ammunition, and any other items you may wish advanced to you."

"That is what you have wanted," St. Clair exclaimed. "That is why I brought M'sieur Davenport here. The British have refused. The Spanish lost power. The Americans have refused. Here is a man who will do what Pyesa hoped for."

It was on the tip of Black Hawk's tongue to say that Pyesa had never wanted white men to come and go freely in Saukenuk. Never before had anyone suggested a store within the stockade. For a long moment he said nothing. Then he walked to the edge of their meeting place. In silence he looked downriver, pointing in the direction he was looking. The others, following his pointing finger, looked at him questioningly.

"That point of land is the place for the trading post. It is easy to reach by water. Platforms can be built out into the river to make loading easier. Trails can lead down to the water on both shores."

"You're right," Davenport exclaimed. "It's a far better location for the post than within the stockade." His eyes twinkled as he added, "And the whites wouldn't have to enter Saukenuk. Or hadn't you thought of that?"

Black Hawk looked at him, knowing he had found a trustworthy friend.

"If you will show us how, my braves will build the post of the round logs as the white man builds," he said.

"That will be fine."

"And here on this spot from which you can see only the willows bending to kiss the waters of the river and the little point and island where the post will be, we will build you a home like the white man's house, at this point where first we friends met."

When on the morning of the next day the two white men departed, Black Hawk was suddenly aware of a great loneliness. But Davenport soon returned and, less than a moon later, the work of building the post began. The wickiup that had sheltered the white trader on his visit transformed into a log house. It became the scene of many a long talk between the white man and the Sauk.

"If our people could only trust each other as we do," Davenport once exclaimed, "there would be no more cruelty on either side." He laughed suddenly. "My father used to say, 'It is better to trust people and be wrong fifty times than to be suspicious of everyone and accuse one man unjustly.'"

Black Hawk did not smile.

"My father chided me because I disliked scalping women and children," he stated boldly, and Davenport stopped smiling.

"Yes, there are many differences in our two peoples," he said. "Does that mean we cannot be friends?"

"I had always thought so," Black Hawk answered, "until you came."

The more he talked with Davenport, the more closely Black Hawk felt drawn to him. Was it wrong to like a white man, he wondered? He knew what Pyesa's answer would have been.

Perhaps if he were to go into the deep woods for a time, he might find an answer. If the Great Spirit truly smiled upon him, it might even be that Watanka would give him some sign, so that he might know what he should do.

That very day Singing Bird told him they were going to have a son.

"That settles it!" Black Hawk cried. "I must learn to teach myself before I can begin to train a son."

"I will bring up your son, Black Hawk. Pyesa always used to say I would know how to make warriors of his grandsons."

"Does that mean you will teach our first-born to tear the wings from butterflies?" Black Hawk asked bitterly.

"Black Hawk!" his wife cried out, almost as if he had struck her.

At once he was ashamed. "I'm sorry," he said. "It's just that I don't know what it means to be an Indian. I don't know how to bring up a son in this kind of world."

"Your son will be as you want him," Singing Bird said. "He will learn to be gentle, but he will learn to kill, for he is a Sauk. But you must know one thing, my husband. He will be brought up as the son of Black Hawk, *not* as the grandson of Pyesa."

"Then let us go to the deep woods," Black Hawk cried. "Let us learn to know ourselves. Perhaps Watanka will tell me what it means to be the son of Black Hawk. He may even tell me what it means to be Black Hawk!"

The troubled chief left Grey Owl in charge of the warriors, with Red Bird as his assistant. White Cloud was still able to handle peace problems, as long as Davenport would be there to work out the trading terms, for he could be trusted not to cheat the Sauk. Black Hawk told everyone he was going to the deep woods to show respect and grief for Pyesa.

He was prompted by a feeling that he must hurry to the deep woods where the truth would be waiting for him.

As he and Singing Bird, holding hands like young lovers, mounted the trail, they came to the plateau Black Hawk had always loved. Husband and wife turned to take a farewell look at Saukenuk. It was then he noticed a long, wide field stripped as clean as any of the white man's fields, just beyond the farther end of the stockade. He frowned.

"I never told them to cut down trees for the stockade," he said. "I told them to bring in dead wood. I must remember to punish whoever did that."

Singing Bird laughed.

"We're going away," she said. "Remember?"

He smiled.

"I'll try not to forget again," he said, and they started off on their long journey.

CHAPTER 12

The large clearing Black Hawk had noticed was not the result of gathering wood for the stockade, nor was it an accident. It had been made by the planning and hours of back-breaking work by a nine-year-old boy named Keokuk and his playmates.

Keokuk was one of the children who had cried out with joy at the sight of the horses Black Hawk brought back from his first victorious sortie against the Chippewas. He had absolutely no fear of them. Indeed, there seemed to be some sort of kinship between them and the stocky little boy. Even the great white stallion that bared his teeth at the approach of the Sauk or Fox braves stood quiet when Keokuk came near. The horse was considered "bad medicine," full of an evil spirit. So, when he allowed the child to caress him, the Indians believed Keokuk possessed some strange power.

When the food scarcity tempted the Council to kill the animals to save feed, Keokuk's father offered to provide for them. It was he, too, who, with the help of his wife and small son, planted the long hillside with alfalfa, which the horses liked so well.

And so most of Keokuk's boyhood was spent around the horses. His young friends, envying his ability which made these fierce-looking animals do his bidding, asked him to teach them his secret "medicine."

Keokuk trained his companions by taking them on long hunting trips. When he discovered they could not use bow and arrow accurately on horseback, he taught them to hang a spear, slung in looped thongs, at the side of the horse. This could be reached quickly and plunged into a bear's neck while passing it at a gallop.

There were many more would-be cavalrymen than horses—less than twenty horses all told. So Keokuk was overjoyed one time when he sighted a herd of grazing wild horses far away. This was at the old Sauk hunting grounds where Pyesa had massacred the Chippewas. Down on the level prairie, Keokuk noticed that many hoof prints led into the Great Canyon. This was evidently the refuge of the wild herd.

When they returned to Saukenuk, Keokuk's head was full of plans for increasing the Sauk herd. He set the boys to work cutting cowhide and buffalo skin into thin strips. These were spliced together to make long ropes and rubbed with skunk oil to make them both tough and pliable. When the group returned to the canyon, each Sauk horse carried two riders.

At the southern end, Keokuk divided his men, sending half of them up along each rim. When they had reached the place where he estimated the wild horses would take refuge that night, they staked out their own mounts. Then, on foot, they traveled to the point just beyond and above the place they sought. Here they wound their ropes around the boles of the great trees lining the canyon and made ready for the night.

As the shadows lengthened, Keokuk's alert scouts heard a faint clatter echoing up the canyon walls. The animals were returning to the waterhole. Even before darkness hid them from the sharp eyes staring from above, many horses had lain down. Others were sleeping on their feet.

Silently, the free ends of the ropes were coiled and flung over the heads of the horses, who were actually caught napping! As the startled animals screamed and plunged, the ropes tightened. With Keokuk setting the example, the boys slid down the ropes to leap on the horses' backs. The moment their weight left the ropes, the boys still on the rim above played them out, as a fisherman gives line to a fighting barracuda.

Keokuk had selected for himself a tall, broad-backed palomino colt, the color of a wheat field in the sun. At the touch of the boy's knees on his sides, a quiver of resentment shot through the horse. He twisted and turned, trying to rid himself of this strange burden. But the boy at the other end of the rope pulled, and the noose tightened. Keokuk hung on. Guided from above, the horse headed for the mouth of the canyon. Keokuk shouted to let go of the rope. It came swirling about him like a lightning flash.

Catching it, Keokuk quickly twisted it around his body and the horse's neck. He was bound to the animal. As they hit the open prairie, he realized, exultantly, that from now on it was a fight between them.

All the other horses were safely tethered by the long neck ropes. But Keokuk's struggles continued. Everyone watched anxiously as the magnificent animal leaped into the air, his white mane and tail flashing. Then, as they watched, they saw the horse begin to run, screaming in fury! Keokuk knew he had won, and his cry of victory joined the horse's scream.

"Waheee-oo! Waheee-oo! Waheee-oo!"

And they were gone—the great horse like a streak of sunlight, with his rider's muscular, bronzed legs against his flaxen sides, the boy's long black hair and the horse's mane streaming out behind them!

Long after darkness had fallen, Keokuk returned. They greeted their leader, who smiled happily as he rode the beautiful horse into the firelight. Tying the rope to a peg one of the boys had driven in readiness for him, Keokuk stood as if to speak, as the horse walked closer to him and nuzzled his shoulder.

"I've decided to call him Golden Starlight," Keokuk told them, trying to hide how much the horse's affection had moved him. "I'll keep him always."

When the boys returned with their twelve fine new ponies and six mares, they found their families discussing the building of the new stockade, ordered by their leader, Chief Black Hawk.

Although there was some objection, most felt there would

be greater safety for all when the two halves of the village were reunited.

"Father," Keokuk pleaded, "since we must bring in dead trees, can't we get most of them in the big field behind our tipi?"

"You need a cleared space for your new horses, don't you? I see no reason why we should not start with that great cluttered meadow."

When the field was stripped, Keokuk planted it with clover and fast-growing low vines, so that it would form a turf easy on the horses' hoofs. It grew quickly.

Then Keokuk began a series of daily training lessons. He organized riding lessons, which he never allowed to become tiresome, spicing them with races and games. He showed them how to ride hanging far down the horse's side, striking at a moving target with knife or tomahawk, so that one day they would be able to outrun and kill a fleeing fox or wolf. He was determined that the Sauk and Fox would become the greatest hunters ever known.

It was the field Keokuk had stripped which Black Hawk had seen as he paused for a farewell look at the beloved village he was leaving for he knew not how long.

The new trading post was not completed until well in the fall. The maize and winter corn had been cut and harvested. The maize, powdered into meal, was stored in calf skins in a long lean-to shed. The squaws did all the work, for the braves were helping build the long, low log house.

George Davenport was as good as his word. He furnished rifles, ammunition, and traps to all who asked for them. The cost was to be taken out of the prices paid for furs and meat brought in by the Sauks. He expected to have to await the coming of spring before any great amount of skins could be brought in. But he had reckoned without Keokuk! He and his hunters were considered too young to be of much use in the building, since the oldest of them had not seen twelve summers! They did not wait for rifles and ammunition.

The day after the opening of the Rock River Trading Post, Keokuk and his followers rode up to its door, deposited the skins of beaver and deer, and even a grizzly bear, on the porch, remounted their horses, and returned to Saukenuk. Davenport found them there when he came to open up in the morning. He was ready for business months before he had expected to be!

News of the great Sauk hunters traveled fast. Soon other white men came to buy skins from Davenport. Some even tried to deal directly with the Sauk. White Cloud and Red Bird, however, issued orders that no Sauk or Fox was to deal with anyone but the friend of Black Hawk. This forced the white traders to buy through Davenport, and his business grew. By this time all the Sauk and Fox hunters were bringing in their spring kill, and the little point of land where the trading post stood had become a busy and populous place. Since he must spend so much time there, Davenport decided to build a house on the point near the post.

Great piles of planks, clapboards, and hardwood boards were poled up the Rock River on rafts from a sawmill at St. Louis. For the first time, the Sauks beheld what seemed another evidence of the white man's magic—milled lumber. And now they saw nails—bits of dull metal that pinned heavy planks together. From beginning to end, the building of the house seemed like a long ceremonial rite. Even after all four walls were in place, and the slanting roof nailed down, there was more cause for wonder. For an enormous raft brought a great metal monster with hinged jaws. It took eight strong men to carry and set it up against one of the tall smoke-eating chimneys. Outside, they waited patiently to see the first stove in operation.

Finally, when everything was ready, there was a big ceremony. White friends of Davenport's came from St. Louis, and even from the Detroit country far off down the winding river. The Sauk and the Fox danced a great ceremonial dance around the new house. Trestle tables were set up, and white man and Indian partook of the white man's food. Although the Sauks found it curiously seasoned, they ate it because it had been prepared on or in the belly of the great black monster, who might be offended if they spurned his brew.

For a long time, the white men and the Sauks lived a friendly, peaceful life together, both equally curious and amused by many of the other's traits and habits, but with complete tolerance.

Red Bird grew soft and fat. White Cloud, growing old, spent much more time at the post than in the Council Chamber. Only Grey Owl kept himself thin and alert, constantly aware of his obligation to Black Hawk. He watched out for possible treachery and kept the braves in readiness. When at last trouble showed itself, it came from a source Grey Owl had not prepared for. It came in a bottle.

So many traders had come to the port that some lived in tents or wickiups for the brief time they were there. Then a white man put up a cook shack, and food was sold. It was soon followed by the sale of liquor.

The whites amused themselves by watching its effect upon the unsuspecting braves, who accepted the drink and the exhilaration it gave them. White Cloud was one of the first victims. They gave him drink after drink, night after night, and waited for him to reach the point of drunkenness, at which he would dance the story of the great deeds of his youth, jumping up and down, pumping his spindly legs, in imitation of the coup dance of the young braves. Then they roared with laughter.

George Davenport was genuinely disturbed. He did not want the Sauks cheated, nor to have anything jeopardize his warm friendship with Black Hawk. He urged Red Bird to have the Council take a firm stand about liquor. Without White Cloud's help, however, Red Bird could do nothing, for, in spite of his loss of dignity, the old man was still Peace Chief. Nor could Red Bird see the harm in liquor, as Davenport did. He even believed that Black Hawk himself would not have disapproved.

When Davenport asked him to send for Black Hawk, Red Bird said that even if he knew in what part of the wilderness the chief had hidden himself, it would not do to bring him from his contemplation for so small a matter.

"Lord, how I wish he would come and help me shoulder this responsibility!" Davenport thought.

At that moment, Black Hawk stood watching the dying sun coloring the lake before him with streaks of pink and cerise—colors he used at the outer edges of his eyes when on the warpath. He felt a part of the world around him, conscious of a great contentment.

Every sunrise for more than a thousand dawns he had sought some sign from the Great Spirit, hoping to be told whether he was to live as his father wanted, with hatred in his heart, or as he himself felt an urge to live, open-heartedly, trustingly. He wanted to know if it was wrong to live contrary to the vow he had made to his father, or even more unworthy to act contrary to his own feelings and beliefs. There had been no sign.

He had spent the days in watching the miracle of his son's growth. They had named him Loud Thunder because of the strength of lung he displayed whenever he was hungry. Black Hawk had reveled in being just a man instead of the Head Chief and Medicine Man of All the Sauk and Fox. His title, the tributes paid to his generalship and his bravery, even his own people, had come to seem very unimportant, here in the deep woods.

Far more wonderful seemed the look on his wife's face the day Loud Thunder walked eight whole paces all by himself!

There had awakened in Black Hawk a new appreciation of the world around him and a feeling that being a part of it was all any man should ask for. He knew that a man must be himself, know himself, and be true to himself.

Suddenly, for no reason, a shudder passed over his body, a definite tremor, and he felt he must return to Saukenuk. It was as if a message had come to him. He knew something was amiss, that someone was suffering because of his absence, and that it was wrong to wait longer for a sign that had not been forthcoming in all the time he had come to the deep woods.

This was the sign he had been waiting for. It was not the right of man to live as animals do, in solitude with their mates and young. Man had responsibilities. Man could think. Man could exchange ideas, such as those that had passed between him and Davenport. Thinking was another of the inexplicable miracles, but it was not an unmixed blessing. It meant that one thought of the well-being of others. It meant carrying one's share of the weight in packing home the kill. It meant swinging as strong a paddle as the next man to help drive the canoe against the current.

With a deep sigh, as if putting from him something that had been very precious, he straightened his shoulders and called out to Singing Bird, "We are going home!"

Many nights they slept under the stars, and many dawns saw them on their way returning to Saukenuk. Their progress grew slower as they neared home, for Black Hawk had the strange feeling that he was leaving behind some part of himself he would never see again. Yet there was an urgency in the pull toward home.

As the trail grew more familiar and Black Hawk recognized old landmarks, he was amazed to see how many wide new trails there were—as if many horses had often passed that way. He thought the trading post must have become a great success. He also thought, fleetingly, that these hard, much-traveled trails would make Saukenuk more open to attack.

A view from the plateau made him gasp. There was the trading post as he had pictured it. And there was what he supposed was Davenport's fine new home. There were other buildings, too. As he stood with his wife and son, looking down at the new village beyond, yet so close to Saukenuk, he was not sure that it was good.

But it was good to see Red Bird and Grey Owl and George Davenport. It seemed no time at all before he was again absorbed by the problems of his people. He had no patience with the drunkards. He established a series of severe and cruel punishments for any Sauk caught with liquor in his possession. He brought forth the quirt, which had not been used in Saukenuk since before Pyesa's time, and he saw to it that the guilty were given twenty lashes in plain view of everyone in the Great Square. Drinking in Saukenuk came to a speedy, though painful, end.

To compensate the braves for this deprivation, Black Hawk and Davenport worked out a program of activities that would encourage friendly relations between the Sauks and the white traders in the little white village that surrounded the trading post. Wrestling, horseshoe pitching, archery and rifle contests and dances enabled the men and women of both races to meet and enjoy each other's company without the inflammatory dangers of firewater. These games and dances were always supervised, and either Black Hawk or Davenport was always present.

Davenport insisted on bringing milled lumber up the river to cover the little house at the river's edge where they had first become friends. It became a sort of sanctuary—a place for him to come to from the post, and to which Black Hawk came to escape the problems of the village. There they could talk of faith and trust and all the vague feelings that Black Hawk could discuss with no one else. After a few moons, Black Hawk had again become Head Chief and Medicine Man of All the Sauk and the Fox, and for the most part, he found it good.

CHAPTER 13

Black Hawk had chosen that day to take his young son on a long-promised trip. Loud Thunder had begged to see the place where the salmon leaped from the rapids in their foolish but gallant attempt to swim against the current. He wanted to sleep under a full moon, as they had not done for nearly two years.

The sun was bright; the crisp air was filled with the pungent smell of sycamore. The morning gave no hint of warning.

They left early. It was nearly noon when a messenger from Davenport arrived at the wickiup to say he had been called away suddenly.

Singing Bird heard, and, understanding the importance of someone being at the post dance that night, went at once to Grey Owl's wickiup. She explained that she felt she could represent Black Hawk at the dance and asked Grey Owl to accompany her. Although he had attended few of the monthly dances and disliked adorning himself with chaps and other concessions to the customs of the whites, he agreed. Crescent Moon, who loved watching the strange antics of the white man's dance and could not go without her husband, welcomed the chance to go, too.

There was an unusually small attendance that night. Besides the fiddler and the trader who played the mouth organ, there were only a dozen white men, two of whom had brought their wives. There were fifteen young braves and not more than ten Sauk squaws and maidens. Everything went smoothly at first.

Crescent Moon was enjoying herself. The strenuous gyrations that left the whites breathless she performed with effortless ease.

She remained cool-looking and placid while the white ladies unashamedly wiped perspiration from their pale brows. She glowed, aware of Grey Owl's approving glances. Everyone seemed to be enjoying themselves.

But this all changed when a white trader made a belated entrance. The cause of his delay was immediately apparent. He had stopped for too many drinks at the little bar that still was permitted to serve whites. At first he seemed only noisy but good-natured in his drunkenness. When his arm remained around Crescent Moon's waist longer than was called for by the needs of the dance, she merely sent a reassuring glance toward her frowning husband. But when he became more affectionate, she grew nervous. She knew how much these dances meant to Black Hawk, that to cause an unpleasant embarrassing scene or risk insulting a white man would destroy the purpose for which they were arranged. So she tried to hide her growing distaste. When the drunken trader kissed her, however, she could not restrain a cry of alarm.

Grey Owl walked across the dance floor, straight to his wife's side. Taking her arm, he released her from the white man's crude embrace. The trader looked at him in bleary-eyed surprise.

"Sho shorry," he mumbled. "Didn't know was your squaw."

Grey Owl walked his wife toward the door. "You had better go back to Saukenuk," he said quietly. "I must remain here."

"You come home too, Grey Owl," Crescent Moon whispered urgently.

"Black Hawk would not want me to leave our women unprotected," he answered.

"Crescent Moon is right," Singing Bird spoke as they reached her side. "There are enough braves here to protect the squaws. If you stay, you will fight, and above all there must be no bloodshed."

Unobserved, the drunken trader had stumbled over to them and now addressed Singing Bird.

"I don't know what yer jabberin' about," he said, "but yer too pretty to look so serious. Ferget this big buck an' dance with me."

Throwing his arms around Singing Bird, he hugged her close.

Sudden rage flamed in Grey Owl's eyes. He had always worshipped Singing Bird, and besides, she was the wife—the only wife—of the Chief of All the Sauk and the Fox. She had been profaned in public! Grasping the white man's hairy arm, he swung him away from the girl his brother had married. The trader lost his balance and sat down hard on the rough floor.

The Indians huddled together, realizing the bad trouble to come. The fury in the trader's face was apparent. Two white men each grasped an arm as he tried to rise.

"Forget it, Sandy," one of them said.

"Forget it!" bellowed the trader. "A dirty Injun pushes me around, an' I'm shuppposed to forget it! Not on your life!"

"Sandy, listen to me," one of the others said soothingly. "You're more than a little drunk, m'boy. Start anything an' you might get hurt."

"*Me* get hurt? I'd like to see him try to hurt Sandy Stapleton. Why—" He tried to wrench his arms free, but his captors held him firmly.

"You were in the wrong, Sandy. Now either get out or go over and apologize."

"Can't apologishe. Don't speak the language."

"He'll understand if you go over and offer to shake hands."

"Let's go over. I'll 'pologishe." They followed close behind him as he weaved toward the quietly watching Sauk.

As he approached Grey Owl, Stapleton stuck out his hairy right paw. Grey Owl remembered that the clasping of hands meant friendship with the white man. He did not want to be friends with this dirty, evil-smelling man, but he thought Black Hawk would wish him to forgive the insult. So he glanced down at the extended right hand and held out his own.

In that instant Stapleton's left arm delivered a smashing hook to Grey Owl's jaw. The Sauk's head crashed back against the door. His eyes glazed as he slid to the floor. The trader was on him in a flash and, before the other whites could stop him, had kicked the ribs of the fallen warrior.

Grey Owl rolled aside to avoid the heavy boot. As his fingers clutched at his stomach to ease the pain, they touched the cool steel of the long knife at his belt. Instantly, he was on his feet. Before anyone had seen the knife, Stapleton was gasping and gurgling as he fell back into the arms of the men who had tried to stop him.

Grey Owl stood silent. He knew Stapleton was dead. Then he looked toward the wall where the Sauk braves and squaws waited for some command to prevent a panic.

"You will go to Saukenuk," he said with quiet authority. "We will all go home. To Saukenuk."

They filed past him in sympathy, but no one spoke, and his stern face gave no clue as to what he intended doing. The white men allowed every Sauk to leave. As the last tribesman passed him, Grey Owl looked down at the two women by his side.

"You also," he said. His wife looked up at him pleadingly.

"I will follow," he reassured her. "Go."

When they had all gone out, he was alone with the white men and their squaws. He was suddenly painfully aware of the great barriers between them, for they could not understand each other's language. He wanted to tell them he would not run away. He wanted to ask them to send for Davenport.

All he could do was point to himself and say his Sauk name, "Owambi," which means Grey Owl to him but nothing to them. Then he said, "Owambi Saukenuk. Davenport."

They nodded. Still no one else spoke. There was nothing more he could do or say.

Turning, he followed the others. He sought out the sleeping White Cloud and told him exactly what had happened and asked the old statesman's advice.

"Wait till Black Hawk returns," White Cloud said grumpily. "It's his fault. Had he not refused to allow the sale of the magic water, there would have been no need for dances. Let him tell you what must be done."

Unhappily, Grey Owl sought Red Bird.

"If I were Grey Owl," Red Bird said, "I should leave Saukenuk this very night."

"Where should I go?" Grey Owl asked.

"As far from Saukenuk as possible—not only for your own sake, but to avoid reprisals."

"I cannot feel that I have done wrong," Grey Owl said. "Why should I leave my wife, my brother, my village? The white men saw the trader attack me. They know it was not I who provoked the quarrel."

"They will not side against one of their own race," Red Bird said.

"I shall wait for Black Hawk," Grey Owl replied.

When Black Hawk and his son returned late the following afternoon, it seemed to him the whole ten thousand inhabitants of Saukenuk were waiting to tell him the bad news.

When at last Grey Owl saw Black Hawk coming down the sloping trail, he went at once to the Long House to await his pleasure.

The chief listened in silence to his brother's account of the killing. For many moments he sat, deep in thought. Then he asked Grey Owl if he knew the name of the runner who had brought the message telling of Davenport's departure. Learning the name, he sent a young brave to bring him quickly to the Long House.

The messenger recalled the message perfectly. A man had arrived at the post with a letter for Davenport, asking him to come to Albany at once. This man had obligingly stayed on at the post to guard the supplies and beg the patience of the white traders until a replacement, who had worked before with Davenport, would arrive.

"He did not say whether this man who will come in his place speaks our tongue?"

"No."

"We must send word to Davenport without delay," Black Hawk decided. "He alone can tell us what to do. Bring me the brave who can ride the fastest horse."

Then the chief summoned the Council, explained the danger, and said that Davenport was the only one who could help them.

"We cannot await the coming of the new man, even though he be trusted by Davenport, for we do not know whether or not he can talk so we can understand."

"To reach Albany, one must pass through the heart of the Sioux country," White Cloud pointed out.

"It is a chance we must take," the Head Chief replied as the courier appeared at the raised flap of the Long House. Black Hawk turned and stared in surprise.

"Is this a joke?" he asked the messenger who had followed the courier into the room. "This is a mission of great seriousness, and you bring me a child to fulfill it?"

"I'm not a child," the youthful courier protested. "I have seen twelve summers come and go."

Black Hawk nodded solemnly.

"Keokuk says I am the best horseman in the country—next to him, of course. And Keokuk says my horse Fleetfoot is second in speed only to Starlight."

"And who is Keokuk?"

The boy's mouth fell open, and he stared at Black Hawk in amazement.

"Keokuk is the best rider, the best horseman, the greatest hunter the Sauks have ever produced."

"Is that, too, what Keokuk says?"

"Yes."

"How old is this great warrior?"

"He is fully grown, Chief Black Hawk. He has seen fifteen summers come and go."

"Gnarled and twisted with age." Black Hawk sighed and then asked, "If he is the best rider, with the best horse, why did he not come instead of you?"

"He is hunting in the hills, Chief Black Hawk."

"Then we shall have to be satisfied with second best. The message I am about to give you must be carried through Sioux territory. They may try to prevent your passage. Does that frighten you?"

"I am not afraid of any Sioux," the boy said proudly. "Has not Keokuk shown us how to use the spear as a lance to kill a grizzly? Surely a well-handled spear will find its mark in a Sioux warrior."

"I should like to meet this Keokuk one day," Black Hawk said.

"Oh yes, Chief Black Hawk," the boy said, his voice squeaking enthusiastically. "You must see him. He is the greatest—"

Black Hawk waved his hand for silence.

"I know," he said, "but we are not dealing with him, but with you. Now listen carefully, for the message is a long one."

He then told the boy what had occurred and explained that he trusted no one but Davenport and begged his friend to return in order to advise them quickly.

As he spoke, he wished that he had learned to write so that he could say more of what was on his mind.

The boy repeated the lengthy message and apparently fully understood its meaning as well as its importance to the whole Sauk nation.

"I'll find him," he said confidently.

Black Hawk laid a kindly hand on the boy's shoulder. "What's your name, boy?"

"Spotted Lizard," the boy said.

"May fortune ride your second fastest horse behind you," Black Hawk told him, and the boy ran from the Council Room.

"Now we must wait patiently," Black Hawk said.

They did not have to wait long. Soon one of the gate guards flung back the door flap of the Long House.

"Chief Black Hawk," he gasped. "There are soldiers at the gate. They seek Grey Owl."

"Go to your tipi, Owambi," Black Hawk ordered his brother. "I shall go to the gate and speak with them."

Once more the language barrier created an insurmountable obstacle. Neither of the two young officers in the buckskins of the U.S. Army Scouts nor the tall, patrician Indian chieftain could make themselves understood beyond the obvious fact that the officers wanted Grey Owl and Black Hawk did not intend to surrender him.

Black Hawk repeatedly mentioned Davenport's name, in the hope they'd understand he was waiting for his friend to return, but they had never heard of Davenport so understood nothing. Finally, in anger and frustration, they left. The gates closed behind Black Hawk as he re-entered the stockade and walked thoughtfully toward his own wickiup.

Next morning word came of the arrival of Davenport's replacement. Black Hawk went at once, unattended, to see the new man. He had to find out if the man spoke the Sauk language. He didn't, but he had brought an interpreter with him. Black Hawk's heart fell, for the interpreter's dialect betrayed him as at least part

Chippewa. The man's name was Mac Wolf Fang. He introduced Davenport's replacement as Mr. Blaisdell. Black Hawk addressed himself to the latter, giving him a complete account of the killing of the Englishman.

Watching the interpreter's beady eyes, he could not tell whether Mac Wolf Fang was translating accurately or coloring the story unfavorably. Blaisdell's face gave him no clue.

"It's a nasty business," Blaisdell said at last. "What do you expect me to do about it?"

Black Hawk thought he detected the trace of a sneer on Blaisdell's curling lips and an answering grin on the face of the half-breed interpreter. He restrained an impulse to reply angrily.

"This matter is of great importance to me," he said simply. "Davenport is my friend. I think he would come to help me if he knew I needed him. Will you send for him?"

The interpreter repeated only the last few words, and Blaisdell laughed. Then he addressed two short sentences to the interpreter, who nodded in agreement before he turned back to Black Hawk with something like a smirk on his wide, flat face.

"The white man says Davenport is very important. He doubts that it would be worth his while to come all the way back because of a brawl between an Indian and a drunken bum."

Once again, as when he had first beheld the stripped, bare countryside, anger against the white man surged up in Black Hawk's throat. He controlled the impulse to slap the infuriating smiles off their faces. This white man was his only hope of help before the messenger reached Davenport. The soldiers wanted Grey Owl, at once.

"Ask him what I must do."

"He says you have no choice. The whites will take him by force if you do not give him up. You will lose everything."

"Possibly not. But many would be hurt if they try."

Then Blaisdell spoke seriously to the interpreter for several moments, and the half-breed nodded. Watching, it seemed to Black Hawk that both of them had become more friendly.

"He says he thinks if Davenport were here, he would tell you to surrender your man to the proper authorities. He says that if he is innocent, no harm will come to him."

"What will they do to him?"

"He says he will be given a fair trial. He says if there were other English present who can swear that Grey Owl was attacked by the white man, he will be released."

"Released!" Black Hawk cried out. "Will he be imprisoned? Why? He is innocent of any wrong! Can they not hear him before they imprison him instead of afterward?"

Blaisdell shook his head sadly as if in pity of the Indian's vast ignorance. It was the interpreter who spoke.

"That's not the way they do things, the dirty whites," he said. "They throw a man in jail first and apologize later if they find he didn't do it. There's nothing you can do about it."

"I will not give him up."

"You'd better. Take my advice. They'll get him one way or another. It's best to do it their way. Besides, it's not so bad really. I've been in jail about nine times. It's just a big open stockade. You eat. You sleep. Not too bad."

"An open space?"

"Yes."

"They don't torture prisoners?"

"No. And your friend Davenport will be back before too long. If Grey Owl hasn't been tried, he can help you get him out—if he wants to."

Black Hawk hesitated no longer. "I shall give Grey Owl to the soldiers."

Upon leaving the post he faced the most difficult task of his lifetime. He had to tell Grey Owl. Grey Owl trusted him. So did Crescent Moon. Possibly their love for him would turn to hate.

He walked swiftly to his brother's wickiup. Grey Owl, who had been pacing back and forth, looked up as Black Hawk entered and read the answer in his chieftain's eyes.

"Don't mind for me, Black Hawk," he said quietly. "I have done no wrong. You and Crescent Moon and Singing Bird know that. That is all that matters. I would not have you or the Sauks suffer because of me. I should never feel free again. It is better so. Take me. I am ready."

Crescent Moon came running to him then. "Not yet," she cried. "Oh, please, Black Hawk, not yet."

"It is better now," Grey Owl said, stroking her hair. "Waiting makes it worse."

Gently he pushed her from him and crossed to Black Hawk's side. "Now," he said. At the door, he turned back to Crescent Moon, who stood with her hands to her mouth as if to shut in the sobs. "The sooner I leave, the sooner I'll return," he said.

Black Hawk walked in silence with him to the gate. The guard swung it open on its silent leather hinges. Grey Owl went alone to seek the soldiers who had come to arrest him. He found them. While awaiting further orders, they were carousing in the bar at the post.

CHAPTER 14

Autumn colored the leaves; winter had covered them with snow; spring thaws changed the usually mild little Rock River to a roaring maniac. Still there was no word from Davenport, nor any message from Spotted Lizard.

Every day Black Hawk's thoughts turned to Grey Owl. Although there was never a word of reproach, he imagined both Crescent Moon and Singing Bird blamed him for the warrior's absence, and that even his small son looked at him with something less than pride.

When the trails became passable, Black Hawk called together eight older braves and bade them prepare for a journey to St. Louis. It was a Sauk custom that if a man killed another accidentally and brought lavish gifts to his bereaved family, he would be forgiven, both by the relatives and the Great Spirit. When no word came from Grey Owl, Black Hawk decided to send a party to find the family of the English trader.

Gaily adorned baskets were filled with turquoise bracelets, leather chaps, and bows and arrows. They were placed into two outrigger canoes, for the Great Trail had been extended to meet the river.

Walking Bear and Naquamse led the little expedition of Council members, who were better able to do things accomplished by talk than by deed.

Black Hawk instructed them to find J. B. Patterson, who spoke Sauk and had seemed friendly. Through him they were to locate Stapleton's family for the presentation of the gifts. They were to find the stockade where Grey Owl was imprisoned and give him messages of cheer from Singing Bird and Crescent Moon. They were to tell him that if he had not returned by the time the pussy willows showed themselves, he, Black Hawk, would come to St. Louis and carry his brother home on his own shoulders.

After the party left, another period of waiting began. Several weeks passed without a word. Then one day Tecumseh, Chief and Medicine Man of All the Shawnee, arrived. He had traveled through hostile country in order to confer with the Great Chief of the Sauk and the Fox.

Tecumseh's straightforwardness won Black Hawk's trust and admiration. He had come, he explained to the assembled Council, to unite the Indians.

"The white man has always outnumbered the Indians," he said, "only because he can summon up great forces in time of need. If all tribes would stand together as one great Indian nation, they would fear our strength. There would no longer be need for scalping and hideous mutilation, which are now our only means of instilling fear in the white man. Our oneness would force them to deal with us as they do among their own tribes."

White Cloud cackled the senile laugh of a man whose brain has been softened by white man's liquor. "You think we should fight side by side with the hated Sioux, or they with us?"

Tears streamed from his eyes and saliva from his quivering lips as he slapped the table in wild amusement. Black Hawk felt shamed that such a man was Peace Chief. He spoke quickly. "Have you talked of this with the Chippewa and the Sioux?"

"Yes," Tecumseh answered. "They see good medicine in the plan. They, too, wondered if the Sauk and the Fox would trust them. They are giving the plan much thought."

"We, too, will give it thought," Black Hawk said.

"Do not delay." Tecumseh now addressed himself only to Black Hawk. "Now, while the whites are at each other's throats, is the time for us to show our strength."

"Who will lead the united forces?" White Cloud asked suspiciously.

"At first I would," Tecumseh replied, "for I speak the tongues of all the tribes and can also understand the language of the English."

"You speak English?" Black Hawk exclaimed. "Will you take a message to a white man for me?"

"Yes," Tecumseh promised. "At least it will be a beginning if two chieftains of such nations as ours are friendly. But again I say: We must forget ancient hatreds. The whites want more land. This village stands in their way. They will try to take your land from you. Soon they will want the land of the Sioux. The Sioux cannot stop them alone, but with the aid of the Sauk, the Fox, the Shawnee, the Apache, even the distant Navajos, the whites will hesitate to attack. Then they would listen to us."

"It might mean peace instead of war," Black Hawk said. As Black Hawk and Tecumseh left the Long House, White Cloud muttered something disparaging, inaudibly.

"I'm afraid you have made an enemy," Tecumseh said.

"No man makes an enemy," Black Hawk replied. "One discovers him. See how difficult it is for us to agree even within our own nation! How, then, can we expect to agree with other nations?"

"We cannot hope to agree." Tecumseh's voice was sad. "We are not like the whites, who do everything together in crowds. Our warriors fight each for himself. The white warrior does as he is told. If we fought together—"

"*Must* there be fighting?" Black Hawk interrupted. "Would they not listen to us if we were united?"

"United we might make them fear us for a time. In the end there would be fighting. You spoke of a message you wanted delivered."

"Yes, Chief Tecumseh. Will you stay with us tonight? My wife and I would be honored. I shall have a wickiup put up for your men and see that they are comfortable."

He ordered this done, then sent a runner to tell Singing Bird that Tecumseh would be their guest. As they walked through the apple orchard, Black Hawk told about Grey Owl and of his helplessness and humiliation in trying to deal with Blaisdell. The message, he said, was for Davenport.

"Davenport has joined the Army of the United States," Tecumseh said.

"That seems impossible! He didn't believe in killing!"

"You surrendered Grey Owl to the Army. Davenport will not take sides against them for you or him. It is my belief that the only good white man is a dead white man," Tecumseh said bitterly. "You have not heard from him because he will not raise his hand to help you."

"I do not believe it," Black Hawk repeated with stubborn loyalty. But he was deeply shaken.

At the wickiup, Black Hawk noticed the surprise in Tecumseh's eyes when Singing Bird, after placing bowls of fish stew before the men, took her place at the table. Most squaws did not sit at the table with their husbands.

Yet, in Tecumseh, Black Hawk had found a man he could trust, and he told of his own doubts—how he hated killing and was troubled by this feeling, as it seemed disloyal to the memory of his father. "I was often tempted to speak of this to Davenport," Black Hawk remarked, "but something within me kept me from unburdening myself to one not of my own race."

"It is just as well," Tecumseh replied. "You would only have incurred his enmity. An Indian who thinks is dangerous to the whites. They talk of freedom, but they mean freedom for themselves and their own gods."

"Davenport used to say the white man wants something for which there is no word in our language. In English, he said, it is called 'power.'"

"You should learn their language," Tecumseh admonished. "Then you could better understand their lust for power. I go soon to see the English. They have spoken to me about bringing some of my Shawnee braves to fight the Americans. If you wish, I will suggest you, too, be asked."

"I would not like that," Singing Bird said.

Tecumseh raised his shaved eyebrows. Indian squaws did not often express their likes and dislikes in the presence of men. But Black Hawk did not seem angered.

"Fear not," he said to his wife, "I shall not go." He turned to Tecumseh. "I've had enough of killing."

"Being with them, you would learn their language."

"The price is too high," Black Hawk said firmly. "I will see that your braves have everything they wish," he added, as they rose from the table. "Then we will go together to your wickiup."

As he spoke, his sharp eyes caught sight of something on the plateau above Saukenuk. There were men moving slowly and warily, wearing the scarlet coats and black tri-cornered hats of the British army!

"They're not British," said Tecumseh, who followed Black Hawk's stare. "They are Indians."

After the first startled glance, Black Hawk recognized Grey Owl's rescue party. All eight were there, but they were carrying a ninth on their shoulders. They were wearing the uniforms of the British—coats open, hats askew, swords clanking at their sides. The one they carried was not in uniform.

Suddenly there was a rustle and a gasp as Crescent Moon was at his side. She, too, had recognized the returning Sauks. Now she clutched at Black Hawk's arm.

"They're bringing him home," she said.

In long strides, Black Hawk covered the space between himself and the bowed head of Walking Bear.

"What did they do to him?" he demanded fiercely. "Is he hurt?"

"Grey Owl is dead," Walking Bear said quietly.

With a little moan, Crescent Moon sank to the rocky path. Black Hawk picked her up and carried her down the trail. As he strode along, he remembered the first time he and Grey Owl and this girl had come along that same path. She had been his captive—a present for Singing Bird. And he had been jealous of Grey Owl, whose body now joggled on the unsteady shoulders of the costumed pallbearers.

"Have the smudge fires lighted," he ordered the guard. "Tell Walking Bear to lay my brother at the foot of the Totem. Then have him and the whole party report to me at the Long House."

In silence Black Hawk carried Crescent Moon to the wickiup she shared with Singing Bird. "Be with her when she wakes," he said quietly. "She will have need of you. My brother is dead."

He laid Crescent Moon upon the buffalo robe that covered the couch of pine boughs. "I don't know how he died," Black Hawk said. "But I mean to find out at once."

When he came out onto the little clearing in front of the wickiup, Tecumseh was no longer there. Black Hawk strode grimly toward the Long House.

CHAPTER 15

As Black Hawk strode toward the Long House, squaws and braves carried loads of wood to the end of the Great Square to be lighted as the fire of death before the body of Grey Owl.

Although the costumes of the men awaiting Black Hawk in the Long House were ludicrous, every face bore the dignity of silent grief. No Sauk or Fox would ever tell the story they were waiting to recount to their chief. Never in the dance around the bonfire, on nights when warriors recorded their deeds of daring, would it be told. And surely no white man would want it printed in the history books his sons would study. For it was a shameful story of trickery and crime—a story that must be remembered whenever men boast of the courage and integrity of the early settlers. Not to belittle their achievements, but to remind us that evil is present in every age and that life is a never-ending struggle between good and evil. When evil wins, it should serve to make us more alert to danger, should show us, Indian or white man, black or yellow, how to avoid the triumph of greed and treachery.

No one wished to tell Black Hawk the story. Outside, the death drums beat their rapid dirge. At last, against the somber background of death and grief, of fires and drumbeat, Naquamse spoke.

He told of arriving in St. Louis and seeking Patterson. As they were carrying great hampers of gifts, it was obvious their intentions were friendly. An interpreter was sent for. Through him, they were told by a short man with much hair on his face that Patterson was in Philadelphia where the heads of the new government had been installed.

They had asked the interpreter to explain to Hairy Face their purpose in coming. They asked for the names of the relatives of the dead trader, explaining that they wished to give them the presents to compensate for the accidental death of their kinsman.

Hairy Face told them they would have to wait. After a long time, he returned with two younger men, named Simpson and Mulvehill, and the interpreter.

"They said they had many prisoners, and it would take a long time to locate the records. We would have to wait, and while we waited, Simpson and Mulvehill would show us the town."

Seeing St. Louis meant going from one tavern to another, sampling the whiskey. Then they were taken to a big tavern with great, square, box-like things called beds. They had slept on the floor and in the morning were very sick. When at last they were escorted back to Hairy Face, he told them the records had been found; that Grey Owl had been tried and found guilty.

Black Hawk asked if the white traders who had been at the post that night had not told what they had seen.

"No," Naquamse answered. "We asked if they had been summoned and asked to speak. The bearded one said they had no way of knowing. Grey Owl, he said, was in prison, condemned to die."

"Treachery!" Black Hawk said bitterly.

"When I told them what had happened at the post—that I had been there—they seemed impressed. They said justice would be done. They told us they would appeal to the judge, who was in a far-off place. We were happy because they believed our story. Mulvehill and Simpson said it would take many days, but we must be patient, and that we should celebrate the words of the great hairy one by another visit to the taverns. That night we cut the feet off the beds so we could sleep on them."

Days passed. At last they were told there had been good news. The judge had been found. When he heard of Naquamse's account, he had gone to the heads of the new government. They had sent a long paper. If the eight Sauk men would sign it, Grey Owl would be released.

Even when the paper was translated, it meant very little to them. It said that the Sauk nation should give up its land to the government of the United States and move to a place called Iowa. The paper said that all lands deeded by the French to Black Hawk's great-grandfather should become the property of the United States and that the government would pay to the Sauk nation two thousand dollars at once and one thousand dollars yearly.

"We said we would not sign away the lands, even though it meant the life of Grey Owl," Walking Bear said.

"They thought we meant we were not willing to sign, and they told us Grey Owl would be tortured unless we did. I explained that the treaty would mean nothing unless Black Hawk, Head Chief, or White Cloud, Peace Chief, had signed it. The whites said they understood, that this was a great trick to be played on the government chiefs in Philadelphia."

So they signed it and asked when Grey Owl would be released. They were told not until the eight delegates had paid their hotel bill and the costs of the drinks at the taverns.

"We protested. We thought we had been their guests. They laughed. They said the inn was claiming a thousand dollars for the damage to the beds. If we did not pay, they would put us in prison until the paper could be sent to you to sign. We told the interpreter to say we had no money, but if they would release Grey Owl, we would come back with furs and skins enough to pay for the drinks and the damaged beds."

"They would not listen." Walking Bear sighed, deeply. "We said, if we were to be imprisoned, they must give us back the paper. They said, 'no.' Then Hair-on-His-Face spoke at length to the interpreter."

"Did you learn the interpreter's name?" Black Hawk asked.

"It was a man named Mac—a renegade Chippewa."

"That evil one!" Black Hawk muttered. "He may have known Grey Owl was once a Chippewa. He may have given them the facts they needed. Did they give you back the useless paper? What did the Hairy One say?"

"He said the government was to pay us two thousand dollars for the first payment. He offered to take this money and pay the debts we had unknowingly created. They would trust us to come for your signing. All we need do was sign another paper saying we had received the two thousand dollars. They would give us a paper that showed all our debts had been paid, and Grey Owl would be released at once. We agreed."

"And then?"

Neither Walking Bear nor Naquamse could bear to tell this part of the story. But at last Walking Bear spoke.

"Then they took us to the prison. It is a great wall of pointed tree trunks standing upright. In front of this wall is a cleared space, surrounded by a lower fence made of split saplings. The gate was unlocked by the guard, and we were admitted to the enclosure.

"One of the gates in the prison wall opened. And there was Grey Owl in the archway. He blinked in the sunlight as if he had been kept in a dark place a long time. When he saw us, his face lighted."

Walking Bear could not go on, and Naquamse, taking pity on him, spoke at last.

"He shouted, 'I knew you'd come! I knew my brother would not let me die! I knew it!' And, still shouting, he began running toward us in great leaping strides. And then the shots came. We did not understand. We only saw Grey Owl leaping in happiness. Then he crashed to the ground. We ran and turned him over. His eyes were staring in surprise, his face covered with dirt. His spirit had passed over."

"Who killed him?" Black Hawk asked between clenched teeth. "Who did this evil thing?"

"Later, at the Town Hall, the Hairy One explained, through the interpreter, that it had been an accident—the prison guard thought Grey Owl was trying to escape. He said he was sorry. What could we say or do? They could have killed us. As we felt at that moment, we would not have cared. But they could have thrown us in prison, and we had just seen Grey Owl come out of that horrible darkness, blinking in the sun. So we said nothing. Mulvehill and Simpson came in. They told us that, since it was our custom to give presents to the kin of a man who had died accidentally by the hand of another, they would like to give us presents."

"They led us to another place and signaled us to take off our chaps. They gave us these cloaks, swords, and head coverings. When we donned these garments, they asked us if we were appeased and would leave St. Louis in peace.

"Then they herded us out of the building as the white man herds his flocks. They mounted their horses and stood by while we lifted Grey Owl to our shoulders. They rode with us almost to the beginning of the forest before they halted. They swept their black hats from their heads and bowed to us. Then they turned and galloped off, back toward the town. It was then we heard their laughter."

For the third time in his life Black Hawk felt black rage flow through him. He fought his anger and wrenched his nerves and muscles to do his bidding.

"You are to think of this no more," he said. "The fault is not yours, nor the debt. The fault is not mine, either, but the debt I now make mine. Have you the evil paper which tells of this thing?"

Naquamse took a folded document from the pocket of his uniform. In silence he handed it to Black Hawk.

"We will meet here at sunrise," Black Hawk said. "You, who tried so hard to save him, deserve the honor of carrying him to the burial grounds. Strip those hated garments from you! Throw them in the funeral fire, and let your thoughts follow their smoke into forgetfulness."

He left to find Tecumseh. The Shawnee Chief was reading by the light of the oil lamp that Davenport had given Black Hawk. For a moment he forgot his grief and anger in wonder at this strange sight.

"Will you help me, Chief Tecumseh?" he asked. "You who can understand the white man's magic of a language that speaks from little black marks upon white paper—help me to understand what this paper says."

But even after Tecumseh had read aloud the long document several times, its meaning was not clear to Black Hawk.

"The Sauk lands described in the French treaty are here said to be fifty-five million acres. An acre is a piece of land about one-third the size of your Great Square," the Shawnee told him.

"And what is a thousand dollars?" Black Hawk asked.

"I know no way of telling you. It is a thousand silver dollars, but it will buy more than a thousand other things, and yet it will bring you nothing you do not already have."

"Is a thousand dollars fair pay for fifty-five million acres?"

"No."

"I cannot believe the white men meant this to be believed."

"Perhaps they intended it only to frighten your men."

They pored over the documents again, and Black Hawk began to learn the meaning of a few of the words.

"I feel I must learn their speech now! At once!" Black Hawk said. "I must never again let myself or my people be so helpless. Did you not say you leave to join the English?"

"Not at once. After I return home."

"Will you arrange for me to join you?"

"I will speak to them when I go. But do not expect to hear from them before summer."

"While I wait, I shall train our braves. They have grown soft, their muscles flabby. We shall make long sorties and stay away in search of new hunting grounds. I do not wish to stay here now."

"That is understandable," Tecumseh said, as Black Hawk walked to the door with him.

As Black Hawk had told Tecumseh, he was determined that the Sauk and the Fox would never again be victims of ignorance, nor dependent on the white men. He looked upon this as a promise sacred to the memory of his murdered brother and threw himself into the task with fierce energy. He sent many bands for great distances over long and difficult trails, but always within the boundaries described in the old treaty with France. Beneath the search for hunting grounds was the determination to restore his warriors to fighting trim.

As more and more new hunting grounds were discovered where game and buffalo were still plentiful, he began sending bigger groups with their families to live from the autumn harvest to the spring thaw in these new sectors. He learned to move as many as four hundred Sauks for long distances with great speed.

As the seasons changed and came around full circle twice without any sign of molestation from the whites, Black Hawk believed that the signing of the so-called Treaty of 1804 had been no more than a cruel private jest to frighten and humiliate the little group who had tried to free Grey Owl. Any lingering uneasiness he had disappeared when once again two white men came asking for him, who, when he met them in what he once called the "Davenport House," again offered grain and rifles for some of the Sauk lands. As they were government agents, and since they did not mention the paper that Naquamse and the others had signed, Black Hawk believed the government had never been told of it.

So his anger against the Americans and their government abated. He became more occupied with the upbringing of Loud Thunder, determined that he should not be harassed by the doubts that had troubled him in his own boyhood. He heard nothing from either

Davenport or Tecumseh, though traders had brought news that the Shawnee's efforts to unite the Indians had failed dismally.

When he had almost forgotten Tecumseh's offer to speak about him to the British, a message was brought by courier from a General Dixon stationed near the Canadian border, asking him to report with as many braves as he could muster. It was more because of the opportunity to study the ways and language of the English than hatred of the American whites that prompted Black Hawk to accept the offer.

One factor that influenced his decision was the education of Loud Thunder, who was now old enough to follow a trail and handle a rifle. Black Hawk thought his son should learn for himself the ways of the whites, for in time he would have to make his own decisions about them.

But the greatest inducement was that the British offered him a treaty insuring that the Sauk land remain in the possession of the Sauk forever, in accordance with the French treaty, if he brought a large enough force to offer a real challenge to the American Army.

Tecumseh must have given an eloquent account of the Sauk chief's bravery, or the English would not have offered such generous terms. Black Hawk recruited warriors from the men he had been training. They were restless, tired of hunting, and ready for adventure. And the old legend that Watanka smiled on Black Hawk still held. Everyone knew that ill would befall those who refused to follow him.

Early in the summer, Black Hawk left Saukenuk, with young Loud Thunder acting as "point" with Red Bird, who was lean and hard-muscled again, running by his side. In commanding the largest Sauk army ever to take the warpath, he felt that he was fulfilling the prophecy that had come to him in the deep woods. Pyesa's eyes would crinkle at the corners in a smile, if he were looking down upon his son. And Black Hawk was content.

CHAPTER 16

White Cloud had nursed a grudge against him ever since Black Hawk, working with Davenport, stopped the sale of whiskey to the Sauks. With Black Hawk away, taking every able-bodied warrior, there was no one in Saukenuk White Cloud need fear.

He lost no chance to speak disparagingly of Black Hawk and to create an atmosphere of fear of the dreadful things that could happen with no one to defend the village. When it was reported that a party of more than two hundred Sioux had been seen approaching Saukenuk, even White Cloud was frightened, for he had no reason not to believe the fears he had been creating in others!

The Council tried to select a War Chief. They were in heated conference when the sentry entered to announce that a youth begged an audience with them. No one remembered his name—Keokuk—until Walking Bear said, "That must be the one who boasted he was the best horseman in the whole country. He must be all of twenty years old."

"Black Hawk's absence leaves us in a desperate position," White Cloud said. "Let us speak to this child."

Keokuk had become a stocky, aggressive youth, bow-legged from much time on horseback.

"The Sioux, I am certain, are responsible for the death of Spotted Lizard, the messenger Chief Black Hawk sent through their country. He was my friend. I will avenge him. I and my company will find the enemy and destroy them," he said confidently.

"When will you be ready to start?" White Cloud asked.

"At sunrise."

"Good fortune ride with you!"

"We do not depend on good fortune. We have ninety-one rifles and know how to use them." And Keokuk strode off.

As the sun rose over the far-off plains, Keokuk and his band leaped upon their horses. When they reached the summit of the plateau that Black Hawk had always loved, they were silhouetted against the dull gray of the morning sky. Even at that distance, eyes watching from Saukenuk noted the short, squat figure with flying hair on a great golden horse.

As Keokuk had expected, he found the Sioux assembled at Echo Lake Canyon. No one has ever known if the whites had instigated an attack by the Sioux on the Sauk nation. All Keokuk knew was that they were Sioux. They had killed Spotted Lizard. He had boasted of what he would do when he met the enemy.

It was the same canyon, scene of Black Hawk's triumph of years before, where young Keokuk stampeded the Sioux. And when, on the following day, he headed for home, each of his braves carried his spear upright, braced against thigh and armpit, the better to show the two scalps adorning every weapon.

At least, so it was told many times in dances around the fire in the Great Square at Saukenuk in the nights to follow. Small wonder that the villagers came to think of Keokuk as their savior. For was this not as great a sortie as Black Hawk's victory at Ashawequa? It showed Keokuk to be a leader of great daring and resourcefulness. It also served to shatter Black Hawk's dream of an Indian League.

At the very moment that Keokuk led his triumphant company into the wide-swinging gates of Saukenuk, Black Hawk, too, was homeward bound. For many moons the Sauks had waited within the British garrison, growing restless under the daily routine with no sign of fighting. The American whites seemed always about to attack, but never did. At last, word came that a considerable force was approaching. General Dixon, in the months of attempted training, had realized the impossibility of teaching his Indian allies to think as a unit. So he wisely decided to use the Sauks to terrify the approaching Americans, and he had them begin a guerrilla warfare, setting farmhouses afire, killing, scalping, and mutilating their occupants.

Black Hawk refused to go on these sorties. It was not what he had come all this distance to do. His men went on these gruesome missions under Red Bird, and for a time, reveled in them. But even they grew dissatisfied.

When it was learned that the approaching American force had turned back—possibly because of those very ruins standing as silent witnesses to the ruthlessness of their enemies—Black Hawk told Dixon he wished to withdraw from this war in which there was no fighting. The amazed general said an agreement had been drawn up between the English and the Sauks. If the Sauks lived up to their side of the bargain, their land would belong to them forever. Black Hawk tried to explain that, according to Sauk custom, warriors were free to leave a leader who could not hold them. It was only when Dixon said the Sauk land would be endangered if the Indian warriors withdrew that Black Hawk agreed to leave all who wished to stay under Red Bird's leadership.

Before starting, Black Hawk sought out Shabbona, a Potawatomi chieftain who had served with the British for some time. Shabbona, a friend of Tecumseh's, shared his belief in the need of an alliance of all the Indian nations. Black Hawk told him that something he could not understand was whispering to him that he must go home. It was the same feeling that had called him back from the pleasant silence of the deep woods. Shabbona understood. He, too, believed in things one could not see or put a name to.

"I wish to leave Loud Thunder with you," Black Hawk said. "He must learn the ways of the English. I want you to see that he becomes fearless and a warrior with many coups, for one day he will be Chief and Medicine Man of All the Sauk and the Fox."

After Shabbona agreed to keep his son, Black Hawk addressed

the Sauk warriors with such eloquence that all promised to stay in Canada with the English. Then General Dixon said that Black Hawk had in no way breached their agreement and allowed him to select thirty braves to accompany him on the homeward journey. He selected thirty of the weakest fighters. In this way he would not break faith with the English general.

Trusting none of his inexperienced scouts, he acted as "point." He had seen no signs of any recent traveler, and, as they were going away from the scene of trouble, there was little reason to suspect a surprise attack. He remembered passing by the shore of a large lake on their journey toward Canada, and he made this his goal for the second night's camp.

The fire had been lighted. The stones for cooking were heating in the glowing coals. The braves were resting. The moon was reflected in the gentle ripples of the lake. Black Hawk wished to be alone, thinking possibly Watanka would speak to him or that the quiet of the evening solitude would bring some explanation of this constant sense of threatening danger.

He walked away from the fire to a little point of land jutting out into the water. He stood with head uplifted, listening, his thoughts turned inward. What he heard was not a voice from above, not the inner promptings of his own heart, but a sharp metallic click, the sound made by the cocking of a rifle trigger. Whirling, he flung himself flat on the soft pine needles. Then a second sharper sound of the hammer striking harmlessly against a cartridge told him that a gun had misfired and his life had been spared.

His sharp eyes caught the gleam of moonlight on metal. He gathered his legs under him and sprang in a great leap toward the wavering rifle barrel. His outstretched arms struck the rifle to the ground and in the same instant were clasped about the throat of its owner. Forcing the man to the ground, Black Hawk knelt beside him, drawing the knife from his belt.

"You win, Black Hawk," said a muffled voice, speaking the Sauk tongue.

"Who are you?" Black Hawk asked, awed by the fierce hatred gleaming in the eyes of the white man at his feet.

"I am Jeremiah Kilbourne, American. I have hated you all my life."

"Yet you tried to shoot me in the back without telling me of your hatred?"

"I was willing to forego that pleasure to make sure that you were very dead."

"I see no reason to be equally overeager," Black Hawk answered. "Before I kill you, I want to see your face. Stand up."

The man obeyed. He was fully as tall as Black Hawk. "Turn," he commanded, and as the white man obeyed, he stared in blank amazement, not at the man's face, but at something hanging about his neck. It was a necklace of eighteen matched bear claws! Black Hawk recognized it at once. He had last seen it in the hands of a lady seated in her carriage as she lifted it with nervous fingers from his outstretched palm.

"Who are you?" Black Hawk asked again.

"Jeremiah Kilbourne, American," the man repeated.

"The necklace. Where did you get it?"

"It was my mother's. She wore it always, thinking it would keep her safe from the Indians. It was the only thing that had not burned—except her hair—her shining black hair—*that* had been... removed, as well you know."

Black Hawk looked steadily into the bitter hate-filled eyes of the American.

"Where did you find her?"

"You wouldn't know, would you? You've burned so many farms, scalped so many women. Why should you remember the one who happened to be my mother?"

"Where did you find her?" Black Hawk repeated.

"I am a scout—spy, if you prefer. I was in advance of the American troops. My parents moved from St. Louis many years ago. Their farm in Canada gave me an excuse to come and go without arousing the suspicions of the British."

Black Hawk was silent. He recalled in every detail the beautiful girl in the carriage.

"Your rifle did not fire," he said.

"First time in my life that's ever happened!"

"Perhaps Watanka put his finger between the hammer and the flint," Black Hawk suggested.

"To save *your* life?" Kilbourne demanded and laughed harshly.

"Perhaps I am not meant to die just yet. There may be something I must do first."

"Well," the American said, "get it over with. May Watanka—if he's interested—give you good aim and a more trustworthy weapon than mine."

"I am not going to kill you," Black Hawk answered. "You have been sent to me as a sign that I am right and my father wrong. I have never scalped a woman or a child. Now I know I never will."

"Well, praise be to Watanka," Kilbourne said jauntily, "if your belief saves my life."

"You are my brother," Black Hawk said simply.

"Black Hawk! Don't you understand? I am a spy. I can't be your brother. What you suggest offers me a wonderful opportunity. I can report every move you make to the Americans. I can—"

"You are my brother. You will not betray me."

The flat certainty in the Sauk's voice silenced the white man.

"The whites killed my brother," Black Hawk continued. "Perhaps if I have a white brother, he can teach me to understand why. To understand is to stop hating. To understand would mean the end of the angry fire that burns in my veins when I think of my brother.

You will teach me to understand. From this moment on, you are my brother. You are no longer Jeremiah Kilbourne. You shall be known henceforward as Osauki."

For a long moment the white man looked into the earnest eyes of the Sauk chief. Then he held out his hand. "So be it," he said. "I am Osauki."

Black Hawk stuck his knife in the thong that girdled his slim waist. Then he walked back to where the rifle had fallen and, picking it up, handed it to Osauki. Still in silence, he turned and began walking toward camp.

The lounging warriors sprang to their feet, but Black Hawk quieted them with a gesture. He introduced Osauki as his brother. Though surprised looks were exchanged, no one dared question him.

Black Hawk and Osauki ran side by side for the rest of the long journey. It was thus they walked down the sloping trail from the plateau to the northern gate of Saukenuk. As they approached, the gate opened and a young horseman on a coal black pony charged through it, riding at a dead run toward them.

"Strange," Black Hawk said to his white brother. "Horses were never allowed inside the stockade before." Even before he had finished speaking, the young brave had reigned his horse to a halt close to them.

"Chief Black Hawk," he said. "Keokuk wishes you to meet him in the Council Room without delay."

Black Hawk's eyes crinkled into a smile. "Keokuk wishes to see me, does he? Is that the Keokuk who once called himself the greatest horseman of the Sauks?"

"It is the Keokuk who is now called Head Chief of All the Sauk and the Fox," the boy replied, and, turning his horse, cantered back toward the gates of Saukenuk.

CHAPTER 17

Numb with surprise, Black Hawk watched the courier disappear within the gates. The mouths of his followers hung open, their eyes stared. Then they all found tongue at once.

"Allow two of us to return to Canada," one pleaded. "Chief Red Bird will bring back all his braves. We'll throw Keokuk and his horse-riding papooses out of Saukenuk so fast their teeth will rattle."

"Yes," cried another. "Let us return for help."

"Our warriors must remain with Dixon long enough to fulfill my promise," Black Hawk said quietly. "Only then can we be sure the lands of the Sauk will be ours forever. When Red Bird returns, it must be with a new treaty.

"Go to your families as if nothing had happened. Find out, if you can, how this thing came about. I will meet you tomorrow at the river's edge. If I am not there, seek Singing Bird to learn what has prevented my coming."

They nodded, realizing that their chief might be in personal danger. "The best way to show your loyalty is to obey orders. Come, we shall go home."

"The King is dead. Long live the King," Osauki said.

Turning to one of the gate guards, Black Hawk said, "Tell Chief Keokuk that Chief Black Hawk will come to him before the sun has reached the halfway mark. I go first to greet my wife."

Without hesitation, the guard started off in the direction of the Long House, then stopped as he realized he no longer had to take Black Hawk's orders.

"If you do not go," Black Hawk spoke, with deceptive mildness, "your chief will sit waiting impatiently too long for comfort."

"Cheers, Brother Mine," Osauki applauded, as he strode by Black Hawk's side to his wickiup.

"You are good medicine for me," the chief said. "You fill me with laughter when I should be weeping."

"No one would guess you are 'full of laughter.'"

"It is something within, not to be highly shared," Black Hawk replied. "Anger and hate are like firewater. They burn and destroy. Laughter is warm yet cooling, like milk drunk while still warm from the cow."

When they arrived at Black Hawk's wickiup, he pointed to a tipi. "Go, Osauki. That was once the tipi I shared with Grey Owl before our weddings. It is your home."

"Home is where the heart is," the other said, his lips curving in a bitter smile. "Remember, I am a white man."

"You are as difficult to manage as the horse I rode when I was a brave," Black Hawk chided. "I disown you as a brother and make you my son. As parent, I shall be better able to chastise you whenever necessary."

"I go to my new abode, Father," Osauki said. Then the returning chieftain sought the welcome of his wife's embrace.

Before he left to meet Keokuk, Singing Bird told him how Keokuk's promotion had come about.

"My father made many think you had failed your people by going to distant places when you were needed at home. When Keokuk returned from his successful sortie against the Sioux, everyone regarded him as a savior. Yet, in his speech of acceptance, he said you must have had good reason to leave, since your record proved your never-failing loyalty."

So Black Hawk's feelings toward the young man who had usurped his position were much friendlier as he walked toward the

Long House. But this friendliness was soon dissipated.

The squat, square-faced young man seated behind the Council table did not rise as Black Hawk entered. The older man took this to be lack of respect. But Keokuk seldom stood in the presence of men taller than himself, for he was uncomfortably aware of his short stature. This, however, Black Hawk did not know.

"We are glad to see you, Chief Black Hawk," Keokuk said, smiling broadly.

There was no one but the two of them in the room. Why then, did Keokuk say "we"? Then Black Hawk remembered Pyesa's telling him that Prince Phillip, the king's son, always said "we" when speaking of himself.

"We realize," Keokuk continued, "that we are in a difficult position. Had you returned with several hundred loyal followers, it might have been possible for you to refuse to accept the wishes of our people. Since you come back with only a handful of braves, you can do nothing but accept the bitterness of humiliation as gracefully as possible."

"We, also, are facing a difficult decision," Black Hawk said mockingly. "We *could* await the return of our loyal followers, remind them of the ancient legend that ill-luck follows those who oppose Black Hawk, son of Pyesa, the chosen of Watanka, then attack the village which is now guarded by a pitifully small"—here he bowed slightly—"but incredibly brave handful of boys playing at being warriors. The outcome can be foretold."

"We would therefore be justified in placing you under guard until your warriors return, then holding you hostage for their good behavior."

"The plan has some merit," Black Hawk replied mildly, "but it has its weaknesses. My men know I would prefer to die or be tortured than to have ill befall our village. If they believed I thought you were bad for the interests of the Sauk and the Fox, they would attack without thought of what becomes of me."

"Let's have done with this fencing," cried Keokuk, jumping to his feet and coming around the table to stand looking up at Black Hawk like a bantam rooster facing an eagle. "I have been selected by our people to act as their Head Chief and Medicine Man. Yet I have not asked you to hand over the otterskin. I am not qualified to act as mentor and guide as a medicine man must. They believe in your medicine. It is best for them to continue to turn to you, not me, for guidance of their thoughts and beliefs. So I ask you to remain, not only as Medicine Man, but also Chief of Warriors, second in command only to myself, for I, too, want only what is best for the Sauk and the Fox."

Black Hawk looked into the eyes of the younger man and believed him. He asked only one question.

"Will you help me keep the vow I made to Pyesa, to risk death, disgrace, and torture before allowing a white man to set foot in Saukenuk—to protect at all costs the lands belonging rightfully to the Sauk and Fox nations from the hands of the Americans?"

"I will agree," Keokuk said fervently.

"Then gladly will I tell my men on their return that you are their proper leader. I will serve as your second in command in war, and I will devote myself, as I have always done, to protect our people from injustice."

"You have spoken well," Keokuk said.

"I have spoken and acted as a true Sauk," Black Hawk said sincerely.

Davenport had been right, he thought. It is better to trust people than to be suspicious. When people are trusted, it brings out what is best in them. With a lighter heart, he faced the future. He thought he was prepared for whatever it might present, but many surprises were in store for him.

The first came with the unexpected return of the Sauk warriors from Canada. Keokuk had placed guards on the parapets, against just such a possibility. True, Black Hawk had agreed to hand over his leadership of the whole nation to Keokuk, but Keokuk was taking no chances. He was well aware that the angry braves might get out of control.

When the guards called out the Sauk alert, Keokuk ran to join them on the parapet. Black Hawk also, hearing the warning, left his wickiup and hurried to find its cause. As both chiefs, standing far from each other, beheld the seemingly endless stream of shouting, leaping homecoming warriors pouring from the woods, their feelings were very different—but both knew that a crisis was at hand.

They knew that if the men were admitted through the gates and were told of Keokuk's rise to power, they would be angry. There might well be a revolt that would destroy the village. If they were assembled in the Great Square, their strength would tempt them to overthrow Keokuk's horse warriors. Yet if Black Hawk crossed the bridge and ran around the parapet to address them from the northern wall, they would assemble before the wall in a solid mass which could easily smash the North Gate.

"Have the guards put down their rifles, Keokuk," Black Hawk ordered, and raced for the bridge, crossed it, and sped through the stockaded village to the farthest end. The gate swung open for Black Hawk, and he ran through it and along the ground toward the oncoming tide of men.

Suddenly Osauki was running beside him.

"Now's your chance, Father Mine," he said evenly. "Keokuk dare not order the guards to fire. Nor can he call upon his horsemen to attack your braves. If he killed one Sauk, his days could be numbered on one finger."

Black Hawk said nothing. He was saving his breath to reach a high place where the men could see him. He did, and then came a great shout.

"Black Hawk!" It was Red Bird, who had first spotted his chief and old friend. Others took up the cry, and all headed for him instead of toward the walls of the village. Then, a tall, lithe figure suddenly leaped toward Black Hawk, and he heard a shrill voice calling.

"Father! Father!"

This was Loud Thunder! The son he had raised in the deep woods in the ways of peace! Feeling as though an arrow had pierced his heart, Black Hawk held his son for a moment in his embrace, while the boy chattered on.

"There were eight of them and two of us, Naromse and I. It was a great fight. You would have been proud of me."

The others gathered around Black Hawk and his son, smiling, hesitating to interrupt the reunion, and Black Hawk felt that this might be a sign from Watanka. No gesture of his could possibly have stemmed the onrushing tide of men so quickly. He saw Red Bird approaching, and he spoke hurriedly to Loud Thunder.

"This is your new brother, Osauki. Tell him of your exploits. I will hear them at home later"—he smiled—"many times, and see you dance their story by the fire." Osauki greeted the boy, and Black Hawk turned to Red Bird.

"We have the treaty, Black Hawk! It is as you wished it."

Black Hawk grasped both his friend's arms in thanks and appreciation.

"It is good," he said. "It was right for us to leave Saukenuk and fight for the British. I have saved our lands." Then he mounted a rock and held up a hand for the attention and silence of the shouting warriors.

Keokuk, watching from the parapet, felt his muscles tense. This was the moment he had been dreading.

"Warriors of the Sauk and Fox nation," Black Hawk cried, and silence fell upon them. "By your bravery we have won our lands forever. The English fathers have given them to us as once our French fathers did. The English have always kept their word. They will keep it this time also. And so Watanka has shown us that it was right for me to lead you far from home to defend what we left behind us. But while we were away, our squaws, parents, and our children were threatened by a danger close at hand."

A murmur of shocked suspense rippled through the listening warriors, and Black Hawk continued.

"Because of the great bravery and daring of Keokuk, the attacking Sioux were defeated. Saukenuk was saved. Your families are safe."

He watched a moment, looking from one face to another. They were listening to his every word.

"They had been badly frightened. It is easy to understand that they thought I had failed them and that Keokuk had saved them. So it is the wish of your fathers, your squaws, and your children that Keokuk be Head Chief of the Sauk and the Fox. I have agreed. Keokuk will serve his people well. I will serve under him. I have—"

He was interrupted by angry shouts.

"We will not serve under Keokuk!"

"Black Hawk is our head chief!"

"Watanka smiles on Black Hawk and brings ill-fortune to those who oppose him!"

Black Hawk raised his hand for silence.

"Keokuk does not oppose Black Hawk," he cried. "Has Keokuk not asked me to remain War Chief and Medicine Man of All the Sauk and the Fox? Hear me! It is my wish that you serve under Keokuk. It is the will of Watanka, the Great Spirit."

An awed hush fell on his listeners, and Black Hawk continued. "Keokuk conquered the Sioux because of the horses. No Sauk or Fox has ever before entered into battle astride a horse. And was it not I, Black Hawk, who first brought horses to Saukenuk? I say again, it is the will of Watanka that Keokuk be our leader. Go now to your families with light hearts, for both our lands and our people are safe.

Peace has come to Saukenuk."

"Black Hawk!" someone shouted, but another warrior cried, "Black Hawk and Keokuk!" and quickly others took up the cry and chanted in unison, "Black Hawk and Keokuk," as they moved toward the stockade.

Keokuk, watching tensely from the parapet, gave a great sigh of relief as he realized that Black Hawk had kept his promise and the danger of revolt was over.

Now Black Hawk turned back to his son.

"Father," said the boy excitedly, "now that you are no longer Head Chief, can you still allow me to adopt Naromse as my brother, or must I ask Chief Keokuk?"

Black Hawk smiled, relieved that the boy thought none the less of him.

"Who is Naromse?"

"He is my brother's son," a familiar voice said. Turning, Black Hawk looked into the face of his friend, the Shawnee chieftain.

"Shabbona!" he exclaimed. "What brings you here?"

"I am returning your son," Shabbona answered. "He was a fledgling. He is now a brave. Naromse is my brother's son. His father was killed in the fighting near Quebec. He sent Naromse to be with me and my son Rainbow Sky. And now we are all here."

"And here you must stay," Black Hawk said. "Come. Let us go to my wickiup."

Red Bird and Osauki joined them, and the three boys walked side by side toward the stockade. Red Bird was still indignant about Keokuk, and Black Hawk was trying to soothe his feelings when Osauki interrupted.

"Father Black Hawk," he said, "if a man with the ill-fortune that seems to befall you is one smiled upon by the Great Spirit, what sort of troubles does he have upon whom Watanka frowns?"

"My troubles are as nothing," Black Hawk answered seriously. "Power and titles are white men's words. Nothing troubles me now. My family is together again. Red Bird has returned safely. My friend Shabbona is here that we may talk further of the Indian League. Our lands and our people are safe. So do not think because I am no longer Head Chief that I feel Watanka no longer smiles on me. He smiles on me and all of Saukenuk."

For more than three summers and as many winters it seemed as if Black Hawk had good cause for his contentment. Keokuk, enlarging on Black Hawk's plans of former years, organized hunting parties in which the whole village went to warmer climates before the snows came. The warriors hunted. The squaws packed meat and kept it under frozen water to keep until the return to Saukenuk in the Month of Apple Blossoms.

Black Hawk traded furs and meat for plowshares made by white men and, benefiting by the farms he had seen, taught the squaws how to harness some of Keokuk's older horses to the plow. Fields of corn and beans, squash and melons were planted. When the crops grew and bore fruit, the Sauk and the Fox found themselves much less dependent on trading with the whites. They had meat and vegetables aplenty and a place to live. The warriors were content to let their war paint dry in the clamshells in which it was kept. The horsemen found excitement enough in the buffalo hunt.

When white traders brought word that the British had been defeated at Montreal, but in surrender had demanded that their treaties with the Indians be lived up to by their conquerors, Black Hawk felt even more certain he had acted wisely in joining General Dixon's forces.

When George Davenport returned to the Rock River Trading Post, Black Hawk was completely happy. All doubts about his friend's loyalty disappeared. Again the warm feeling passed from man to man as they clasped hands.

Davenport had aged and seemed tired. No one would have guessed he was sixteen summers younger than the tall, hard-muscled, slender Black Hawk.

Black Hawk told him of Grey Owl's arrest, of the treaty of 1804, and of his brother's death. Davenport's exclamations of shock and horror at what had happened convinced Black Hawk of his complete innocence of any complicity in the tragic farce. And the fact that the trader did not know about it reassured Black Hawk in his belief that it was not official. For Davenport had been a major in the Army at the time. Would he not have heard of any official treaties made by his government with the Indians? Black Hawk thought so.

They fell into their old custom of meeting at the little house, for they had much to tell each other.

Davenport told of his unsuccessful attempts to better conditions for all Indians. He told of having met with Tecumseh and urging him to even greater efforts to unite the Indians so that they could be bargained with, instead of having to settle all disputes by fighting.

"That's one of the many things I've been wanting to talk over with you, Black Hawk. You're the only one who can unite all the Indian nations now that Tecumseh is dead."

"Tecumseh dead?" Black Hawk exclaimed. "I did not know. When...?"

"He was killed near Quebec in 1813, just before the war ended," Davenport said.

At another meeting, Black Hawk introduced Osauki to his friend and was surprised that the two white men did not like each other. Another time he took Loud Thunder to meet Davenport. The boy and the older man responded to one another immediately. This was even stranger, because Loud Thunder spoke of nothing but his proudly displayed scalps and his deeds of daring.

"Pyesa used to say Singing Bird would raise fine braves," Black Hawk said when the boy left.

"She has raised a fine warrior in that son of yours."

"Yes, but he behaves more like Pyesa's son than mine."

"Do you wish that he were a reluctant warrior like yourself?" Davenport asked. "Do you want him to be tortured by doubts as you have been all your life?"

"Is it wrong to want to reach toward the light? Even animals do not mutilate their kill except in the eating of it. Is the pleasure man gets from it right? I know not. Perhaps in my son lies the long-awaited answer from Watanka."

"If you could carry on Tecumseh's work, the whites would negotiate with you, and there would be no need for further fighting."

"I try. Shabbona, whom you have not met, is even now visiting with the Shawnee, Neopope, he who is called 'The Prophet,' to find out whether the Algonquin and the Shawnee and the Sauk might make a small beginning—a step toward uniting the Indian nations."

"I don't think highly of this so-called prophet," Davenport replied. "He is a fake medicine man, Black Hawk. Beware of him."

"He tells the meaning of dreams," Black Hawk said obstinately.

"You don't need 'The Prophet' to tell the meaning of your dreams, old friend. They are good dreams. Trust in them."

"It is not easy to tell the true from the false," Black Hawk answered.

"That reminds me," Davenport said. "What makes you trust your white son, Kilbourne?"

"Only his complete honesty with me from the beginning. He tried to kill me. When he failed, he warned me that he was a spy for the Americans."

"Fine qualifications for a son." Davenport laughed. "I wouldn't trust him if I were you."

"You have changed. It was you who urged me to trust people."

"Perhaps I have changed."

"Osauki has never lied to me in all the days I have known him," Black Hawk said.

The two men lapsed into silence. Davenport was thinking of the impossibility of penetrating the mysterious ways of the mind of another man. After some time, Black Hawk spoke his thoughts aloud.

"We almost quarreled. We must not. For if we who are friends quarrel, what chance is there for others, less close, to get along together?" His eyes closed. Black Hawk was content.

"Strange what one sees with closed eyes." Black Hawk spoke in a trance-like voice, as if he were gazing into the future. "I see a sort of pattern. And yet it is not complete. Had I not brought home the horses, Keokuk would not now be Head Chief of All the Sauk and the Fox. Had you not left the trading post, Grey Owl might still be alive."

"He would be! I could have exerted my military authority to have him tried at the post. I'd never have allowed them to take him away!"

"I know. And the so-called treaty which for so long worried me would never have been signed for the English. It is like the patterns in the baskets our squaws weave. We are each a bit of straw, colored by beet juice or walnut stain. The straw is woven into place, itself meaning nothing, but forming part of the design. Only we never see the basket finished. We never know which straw we are. We can only hope that it will one day be useful."

CHAPTER 18

It was in the Moon of the Falling Leaves in the year white men called 1831 that Osauki disappeared. Everyone at Saukenuk was ready to start at dawn the next day to begin the fall hunt. Black Hawk entered the white man's tipi and found it stripped of his belongings. He sent runners in search of Osauki to the village of the whites which had grown up around the Rock River Trading Post, but he was nowhere to be found.

So Black Hawk started without him, sure he would join them later at the Missouri hunting grounds. But, as the winter progressed, he was forced to admit that Osauki had run away.

Loud Thunder and his adopted brother, Naromse, asked to learn to ride, and Keokuk himself assigned horses to them and supervised their training. By the time the hunt was over, both had become good horsemen and won the admiration of their Head Chief.

On their return journey in the spring, White Cloud fell ill and died. Although he had been hostile to Black Hawk for a long time, he was Singing Bird's father and entitled to honor and respect in death. He was carried back to Saukenuk on the shoulders of four braves.

Black Hawk, acting as "point" for the last time, came alone to the plateau above the village. To his amazement, he saw a stockade as large as the two that surrounded Saukenuk standing where once there had been a heavily wooded hilltop.

He was about to return to tell Keokuk of this startling development when someone behind him spoke.

"Quite impressive, isn't it?"

Black Hawk recognized the sardonic voice of Osauki.

"What is it?"

"They'll tell you it's the new government trading post," the white man answered.

"I will not ask where you have been nor why you left without a word. Nor will I ask you how you know what 'they' will say. I say to you: Go. Tell them that we trade only with the American Fur Company, which our friend Davenport heads. Say that they are on ground belonging to the Sauk and the Fox without permission. Tell them to leave."

"They will not leave," Osauki answered.

"Keokuk will force them to. We are protected by the word of the English."

"They will claim that the land is rightfully theirs by reason of the Treaty of 1804."

"Fools!" Black Hawk cried. "Do they not know that treaty is worthless—that it was never signed by me."

"Perhaps it would be worthless had not Naquamse and the others signed a paper acknowledging receipt of two thousand dollars as a token payment to bind the treaty."

"That money was to pay for damages they had wrought in drunkenness invoked by the whites."

Osauki smiled cruelly as a look of horror came into Black Hawk's eyes. All these years he had thought his people were safe. Now his gravest fears had come alive to harass him.

"Don't expect help from your friend Davenport," Osauki warned. "He can do nothing for you now. He's been offered a Brigadier Generalship in the Army. He will command the Illinois Militia, which is even now being recruited and enlarged, in case you make trouble."

"You lie," Black Hawk said quietly.

A ruddy flush colored the white man's cheek. His hand dropped to the pistol at his belt. Black Hawk, without moving, stared at him unflinchingly, and Osauki's hand fell away from the gun butt. He laughed.

"You spared my life once, Black Hawk," he said. "I return the compliment."

"You cannot kill me," Black Hawk replied. "It is not the will of Watanka."

"You may fool your superstitious braves with that nonsense, but not me. I don't believe in your Watanka. Your faith is both touching and ridiculous." Osauki continued, "Don't you know when your luck has run out? That stockade across the valley is no trading post. Look closely and you will see openings in the walls. Cannons will poke their noses through those holes if you are obstinate. My life would be forfeit if they knew I'd told you, for they plan to take Saukenuk unawares."

"How do you know this?"

"I am a spy. I have always been a spy. My loyalties are not divided, Black Hawk. Men at your command burned down my father's house and scalped my mother."

"Not at my command!"

"So you say."

"I do not lie. But it is important, for I owe you much. I hoped to soften your hatred of us by kindness. The hatred went too deep, but not much too deep, else you would not have come to warn me. Now you will return to the false trading post, and you will tell them that no white man will enter Saukenuk without my permission. Tell them Black Hawk will fight, and so will his two thousand warriors."

Kilbourne looked at him steadily, and the ironic smile left his lips.

"This is goodbye, Black Hawk. At least I hope it is. For if we meet in battle, or if there be fighting of any kind and we meet, I shall be forced to kill you."

"You will never kill me, Osauki. Watanka has spoken."

Kilbourne frowned angrily. "Let me give you one last warning," he said. "Don't go to Davenport. He is honor bound to take you prisoner."

"Prisoner!" Black Hawk exclaimed. "Shut me in a prison as Grey Owl was caged! Kill me, they may. But prison is not for Black Hawk!"

"They know there would be an uprising if you were killed. They want you alive."

Black Hawk smiled. "Then sparing my life just now was less an act of gratitude than one of wisdom," he taunted the white man.

Osauki's face twisted into the familiar crooked grin. "Funny thing," he said. "I like you, Father Black Hawk." And he strode off into the woods.

Black Hawk knew the whites would not attack before attempting negotiations, so there was no need to wait for the others. He would go to see Davenport, taking the shortcut through the apple orchard to the river.

As he came to the place from which he could see the "Davenport House," he noticed that the door stood ajar. Davenport was home!

As he climbed the well-worn path, the door was flung wide open, and a man stepped out onto the veranda. He swung to his shoulder a long-barreled carbine.

"Halt! Stay where you are!" he commanded.

"I am Black Hawk," the warrior called, speaking in his own tongue. "I built that house. It is mine. What are you doing here?"

"Sam," the man called, and another man appeared upon the veranda. "This Injun says he's Black Hawk!"

"The great chief, all alone, wearing no headdress, no nothing but a loincloth!"

They shouted with laughter.

"Get along, you drunken Injun. There's plenty of liquor in the town if you've got the wampum to pay for it."

Bewildered, humiliated, and helpless, Black Hawk turned quickly and took the longer trail toward the post. As he turned, his foot caught in a hidden root, and he stumbled. The men burst into loud guffaws. The sound of their laughter lent wings to his feet as he sped down the steep path toward Rock Pointe—and Davenport.

But he did not have to go to the post, for he saw the familiar stoop-shouldered figure of his friend on the loading platform. There was a barge moored at the dock, and Davenport was supervising its loading. Black Hawk broke into his loping run. His footsteps sounded on the planking of the pier, and Davenport turned.

"Davenport!" he cried.

Davenport gave a quick, warning glance toward the men on the barge below him.

"Running Deer!" he cried in English. "You have come to show me heap big beaver dam. Yes?"

Black Hawk almost laughed aloud to hear Davenport use the pidgin English most whites used in talking to an Indian. But he knew Davenport was trying to keep his name from being spoken in front of the two men.

"Heap big beaver dam," Black Hawk answered. His spirits soared. No dreaded change had occurred here. Davenport still offered the same warm friendship.

"Can't talk here," he said in Sauk. In English he added, "Can show me in canoe?"

Black Hawk nodded, and Davenport told the men he wanted to explore a place where the Indian had told him beaver were plentiful, saying he would return shortly. They accepted his explanation and continued loading the barge. Davenport walked along the pier to the mainland and then down to the river shore in silence. They got into the canoe. In rhythm their paddles flung the bright spray into the spring air as they paddled, still in silence, to the bend of the river and passed beyond sight and hearing of the men on the barge.

"Now," Davenport said without turning.

"There are whites in my house," Black Hawk said. "What is the meaning?"

"They bought it from the government. They have a deed for it. But they'll be out of there in another moon. I've bought it back from them—for you."

"How could they buy what wasn't for sale?"

"The government claims the old false treaty is in effect. Someone has stirred up hatred of you in Washington where the seat of our government is now," Davenport explained. "They are angry because you fought for the British. They wanted an excuse to set aside the British treaty, and someone, possibly White Cloud or your loving son, Kilbourne, gave them the information about the St. Louis papers. They claim those papers take precedence over the later agreement with the English and make it valueless.

"I'm a rich man, Black Hawk, as the white men figures riches," he went on. "I tried to buy all of Saukenuk, and a thousand acres surrounding it. I intended giving it to you. I failed. They would only sell to me if I agreed no Indians would ever be permitted to live on the property. I *was* allowed to buy the 'Davenport House' with two acres because I said it was for my own use. I'll take title within a month, and Simpson and Mulvehill will be out on their ears the next day, and it will be yours again."

"Simpson and Mulvehill!" Black Hawk exclaimed. "The two men who tricked Naquamse! They have been dwelling in that house? They will not be alive when the moon passes."

"Black Hawk!" the trader said sharply. "You must listen and heed my advice. Believe me, I share your feelings. But any hostile act on your part is the only excuse they need."

"And if I do nothing?"

"I don't suggest that. I know you too well. But wait. They will do nothing for a long time. The new trading post is really a fort. In Washington it is called Fort Madison. Men are brought in almost daily in the guise of traders and are trained behind the high walls. They will make no move now, believe me. They are not ready for a show of strength. With your two thousand warriors, you would withstand any siege, and Keokuk's horsemen could make sorties with disastrous effect on them."

"What would you have me do?"

"Pretend you do not know there is anything amiss. Be on the alert and go about the usual spring tasks. Plow your fields. Plant your alfalfa, your corn, and your vegetables. And wait. They will first come with words of peace, hoping you will be frightened into signing the old treaty. Hoping, too, that you will agree to lead your people across the Mississippi River to the western shore and never set foot east of it again. They will offer you a grant of land in Iowa and urge you to go in peace and live in comfort. I know what your answer will be, but they do not. Nor do I know Keokuk, who, after all, is Head Chief of All the Sauk and the Fox."

"Keokuk has given me his promise that he would help me keep the vow I made my father. It was on that condition I agreed to ask my warriors to serve under him when they wished to overthrow him. Keokuk will agree that no white man will occupy Sauk land."

Davenport was silent for a moment. "I think we had better go back now. No one must know you have seen me."

"You leave today?"

"Yes."

"You will be a general?"

"No, I'll keep my present reserve rank: colonel."

Black Hawk said nothing as their paddles dipped and rose in rhythmic unison for several strokes before Davenport continued.

"I tendered my resignation to avoid having to take charge of the garrison. It was refused. So I asked for a transfer, which was granted. I am joining the Quartermaster Corps, engaged in distributing supplies but far removed from all fighting. I shall never fight you, Black Hawk, for I believe right is on your side and that your people's treatment at the hands of men of my race is a shameful blot upon our honor."

"My faith and trust will never falter," Black Hawk assured him with a light heart. "I have known one white man who can be trusted."

As they beached the canoe, Davenport waved to the men still working on the barge.

"I glad we go together to beaver dam," the trader said in English. "I'm sure many beaver will be caught there. Good hunting." Then he raised his arm straight out before him and said solemnly, "How, Running Deer."

Black Hawk felt warmth and laughter bubbling up inside him. With a face as expressionless as a piece of driftwood, he raised his arm similarly and said, "How, Davenport."

CHAPTER 19

What followed was exactly as Davenport had predicted. The squaws completed their planting. Keokuk's horsemen trained on the racing field. The young braves trained in the Great Square. Both Black Hawk and Keokuk believed they could withstand a lengthy siege. There was no sign of trouble brewing.

But in the Month of Roses, three soldiers rode up to the North Gate of Saukenuk. Word was brought to Keokuk they were a General Gaines and his two aides, demanding admission. Keokuk sent for Black Hawk.

"Let us admit them with all outward show of friendliness," Keokuk suggested.

"You and I have sworn no white man is to set foot in Saukenuk," Black Hawk protested.

"It is wiser to forget a vow that gives them knowledge of us that we would keep hidden from them."

"It is never wiser to forget a vow," Black Hawk retorted angrily. But Keokuk, who was Head Chief, ordered the guard to admit the visitors. Thus the first white men since St. Clair entered Saukenuk.

In the Council Chamber, General Gaines presented a copy of the Treaty of 1804. Through an interpreter, he pointed out that it said that, within a period of twenty-five years, the Sauk and the Fox agreed to move from Saukenuk to a place reserved for them in a state called Iowa. He said the time limit had been exceeded by nearly three years. He said that the new Great White Father at the head of the government wanted the Indians to move out of

Saukenuk within one month.

No one spoke. Their silence angered the general.

"If you do not comply," he said sternly, "we shall be compelled to use force."

Still no one spoke.

The general's ruddy face turned a deeper red. "Why don't they say something?" he shouted. The interpreter translated the question.

"When the teeth are closed, the tongue is at home," Black Hawk replied.

The general rose. "See that you're out of here before the end of the month!" he shouted, and all three white men left Saukenuk.

On the twenty-ninth day afterward, General Gaines returned, saying that every Sauk man, woman, and child must be out of Saukenuk by dawn of the day after the next dawn. If they went peaceably, outriders would be furnished to protect them as they marched through Sioux territory to the Iowa plains that had been reserved for them. He painted a glowing word picture of the beauties of the Iowa countryside and the fruitfulness of the soil.

"Our soldiers will help you put up your wickiups," he said. "You can lay out the town as an exact copy of Saukenuk."

"Is the country flat and good for riding?" Keokuk asked.

Black Hawk gazed at him in amazed horror.

"It is wonderful for riding," the general's aide replied.

"Will the government pay us each year?" Keokuk asked.

"Keokuk!" Black Hawk cried angrily.

"You will be paid more than the one-thousand-dollar annuity promised by the treaty," General Gaines replied.

"We will consider the matter," Keokuk said.

"Time for consideration is past," the general exploded. "You will be out of here by dawn, day after tomorrow, or every man, woman, and child will be massacred. The big guns of Fort Madison are trained on Saukenuk, and our forces stand ready to attack. We will return tomorrow afternoon for your answer."

The general and his aides streamed out of the Council Chamber.

"Since White Cloud's death, I am Peace Chief as well as Head Chief of All the Sauk and the Fox," Keokuk said before Black Hawk could give expression to his anger. "This is a matter on which we should hear from our people as well as the Council."

"Keokuk." Black Hawk arose and glared down at him. "Do vows and pledges mean nothing to you? I won for you the loyalty of my men. I could have taken Saukenuk when my warriors returned. You swore you would never surrender Saukenuk to the whites. Have you forgotten?"

"Pyesa is dead. Have you forgotten?" Keokuk mocked him.

"The white man has tried for many moons to pit us against each other," Black Hawk said, his voice choked with fury. "He caused the Sioux to fight the Sauk, the Osage against the Muscow, the Algonquin against the Ute. Divide and conquer! It was less costly for them to have Indians kill each other than to have to fight them themselves. It is the Indian, not the whites, who has conquered the Indians! I have long known this. That was why I allowed you to take over the government of our people. I wanted nothing to divide us and so make us vulnerable. But what the whites have failed to do to the Sauk and the Fox in all this time, you have done in one dreadful moment. I will not give up Saukenuk to the whites without a struggle. This I have sworn, and this vow I intend to keep."

"You have spoken," Keokuk said without rising. "Now will I speak. The great tide of white men sweeps over us. We are a doomed nation if we try to swim upstream as the foolish salmon do. Better to go with the tide and save lives and maintain our existence as a nation. I shall take all those who will follow me and go to Iowa.

Once there, we can rebuild our defenses. We can strengthen our nation. Later, perhaps, we will be strong enough so they will be forced to negotiate with us. We may then recover our beloved Saukenuk."

Naquamse arose. "When chieftains disagree," he said, "there is but one course open. This must be put before our people."

"So be it," Keokuk said, and Black Hawk nodded, although he knew Keokuk had the eloquence he lacked.

The setting sun of that day saw the Great Square filled with the people of Saukenuk. Black Hawk stood on the platform before the totem pole. Keokuk, seated on his horse, looked every inch the warrior and leader as he sat astride the beautiful palomino.

Black Hawk spoke first. He urged every warrior to defend the home of the Sauk, to stay and fight with him even if it meant death. He reminded them that Watanka smiled on the followers of Black Hawk and frowned on his enemies. Shouts and assurances of loyalty, even unto death, came from the warriors. No sound came from the squaws.

Then Keokuk spoke, describing eloquently the beauties of the country to which the white man was prepared to escort them. He pointed out that to die for Saukenuk was both foolish and needless. In ringing tones, he urged them to follow him to safety and prosperity.

And now it seemed the whole nation found its collective voice. Squaws, old men, and children joined in the cry that thundered over the Great Square. Keokuk smiled and held up his hand for silence.

"Those of you who would follow me go to your wickiups," he said. "Pack your belongings and prepare to leave by tomorrow's dawn. Those who would follow Black Hawk to certain death remain where you stand."

The movement that had begun swelled into a great wave as those who chose to follow Keokuk turned toward their homes. Black

Hawk's followers had to fight to keep their feet and were left like scattered bits of flotsam on the beach at ebb tide.

Black Hawk stood for a long moment gazing down upon them. There were perhaps two thousand persons left of the ten thousand who had filled the Square. Of these, there were no more than four hundred warriors. He hid his bitter disappointment and raised his hand for silence.

"We are the fortunate. We are the favored of Watanka," he said. "The warriors and braves will remain here. The others will go to their wickiups and await their men."

When the women had left, he told his warriors to remain within the stockade till all Keokuk's followers had departed. Then, if they were attacked, the squaws would guard the parapets, and the warriors remaining on the alert would make quick rushing sorties from both gates at the same time.

Keokuk sent a runner to the fort to tell them of his decision, but to say nothing about Black Hawk's. So the white general arrived at dawn with a force of two hundred outriders, expecting to escort the entire population of Saukenuk on their journey toward the west.

The North Gate opened, and the procession surged out as if a dam had burst. There was no possibility of a single soldier entering the village against that mass of bodies. This Black Hawk had foreseen. The South Gate was heavily guarded, and the sentinels walked the parapets all around so that there was no danger until the last of Keokuk's followers had gone.

The sun was well up. Thousands of Sauk and Fox had climbed the trail and disappeared beyond the rim of the plateau, taking with them all but a few of the white horsemen, who served as both guards and shepherds, by the time the last squaw had left the gate. Then Keokuk, on Starlight, accompanied by fifty chosen warriors, rode forth to act as a rear guard. The remaining outriders joined Keokuk's riders. Only General Gaines noticed that, after the last horsemen had ridden out, the gate was closed from within. Realizing that there must still be someone there, he spurred his horse to gallop after the rapidly disappearing outriders.

"They're not all gone," he cried. "We've been tricked."

He knew he could not recall enough outriders to storm the gate without leaving Keokuk's warriors unguarded. His little force could be wiped out. "March!" he shouted. "See that none come back. When you are ten miles along the trail, collect their arms. If they try to come back, shoot to kill."

Then he galloped back toward the gate. "You in there," he shouted. "Whoever you are, and however many you may be, we'll come back at sunset. There will be no more tricks, or we will consider our agreement broken. We will send a force after the others and mow them down, if you decide to put up resistance."

He signaled his officers, and they galloped after him to Fort Madison.

Black Hawk called a meeting of his chiefs. As he looked around the circle of faces, his eyes glowed with the excitement of a forthcoming fight calling for the matching of wits as well as strength. He hid the sorrow in his heart, for although Red Bird and Naromse had stayed to fight by his side, Loud Thunder had gone with Keokuk.

"When the white man returns, I will meet with him outside the gate," he said. "They do not know how few we are. If they will leave Saukenuk alone, I will sign an agreement giving them all but a thousand acres of our land and agree to remain at peace so long as we are unmolested. Further than that I cannot go."

The others agreed, and Black Hawk ordered a fire built in front of the totem pole. "All those who can move arm or leg will dance tonight. If they search us out with their far-sighted spyglass, they will think there are more warriors than there are."

The fire was lighted, and shortly afterward the gate guard sent a runner to the Long House announcing the arrival of the general. Red Bird mounted the parapet on one side of the gate, Naromse on the other. As the gate opened to allow Black Hawk to pass through, he heard two clicks and knew that two cocked rifles were pointing at the general and his men.

"We have not come to make terms with you," General Gaines said.

"You will hear me," Black Hawk said. "The rifles aimed at your heart command at least that. We wish war no more than you do. But we must be heard."

Then he outlined his proposal.

The general shook his head. "If you are not out of here by dawn," he said, "your village will be destroyed by shellfire and mortar and flamethrowers. By nightfall there will be nothing left of Saukenuk and no one alive within its smoking ruins."

"You are a brave man," Black Hawk said, "to be so heedless of the rifles on the parapet."

"Kill me if you will," Gaines replied. "It will only bring the whole Federal Army down upon you. Saukenuk must surrender. There will be no Sauk or Fox east of the Mississippi tomorrow night."

"You force war upon us," Black Hawk said quietly.

"Remember, not only you but the others who followed Keokuk in good faith will be wiped out. If you resist, there will not be a Sauk or Fox alive east *or west* of the Mississippi."

"Our answer still is no," Black Hawk answered.

General Gaines nodded. "You haven't a chance, Black Hawk, you poor deluded, gallant fool!" But the interpreter did not translate his words, and Black Hawk went back inside the stockade.

Singing Bird was waiting as the gate closed.

"Our son is with the others," she said.

"You heard?"

She nodded.

"I must not allow that to influence my decision."

"What *should* influence it, then?" she cried. "Does nothing mean as much to you as your pride? Does no one living mean as much to you as the dead?"

"Leave me," he answered. "I must face this decision alone."

After more than an hour of uncertainty, he called Red Bird, Naromse, and his other loyal officers to him.

"I have asked the Great Spirit for guidance," he said. "And I have reached a decision. We must abandon Saukenuk. We are four hundred against many times that many. Here we cannot hurt them. If we go into the woods toward the north, we can harass them. We can burn the farms of the whites, fighting as we fought in Canada. We can instill great fear in them and inflict far more damage than we could here."

Black Hawk saw relief flash across the faces of his listeners. This was the kind of fighting they loved.

"There are two thousand of us," he continued. "Everyone be ready to leave by midnight. They are probably watching the gates but not the bridge. We will cross the bridge and descend the far bank to the water's edge. The squaws and children and elders will go by the outriggers. The braves and warriors will run along the southern shore. We will go upstream, heading toward the deep woods of the north. When we have put a safe distance between us and the Fort, we will strike out across the land toward the clearing on the shores of the Lake of the Crying Geese. There we will find room for tipis for our families and the surrounding forest deep enough to hide our braves. Once encamped, we will leave the squaws who can shoot on guard, and the braves will go forth on sorties."

That moonless midnight Saukenuk was the scene of a large evacuation. Two thousand persons crept across the hard-baked dust of the swaying bridge to the farther shore. In silence they climbed into the canoes. The paddles made no sound as they knifed the still waters. Like darker shadows amid the darkness of the overhanging trees, the gallant remnant of a proud nation was swallowed by the blackness of the night.

When a force of a thousand infantrymen and two battalions of U.S. Cavalry arrived at Saukenuk at dawn, they found both gates swinging wide and no living soul inside the two stockades. At the foot of the totem pole, where the bodies of Grey Owl and Pyesa had once lain in state, a cat sat calmly washing her face.

CHAPTER 20

"The warriors grow restless, Black Hawk," Red Bird said. "They say you are afraid to attack. I've silenced two such curs with my clenched fist. I dared not kill them, for we shall need every man if the time comes."

"It will come," Black Hawk spoke gravely. "I have not lost my courage. The whites did not follow us. This means they thought we intended to join Keokuk in Iowa. If any scouts have been sent in search of us, they have returned and reported failure. Once we begin burning farmhouses or attacking small parties or companies of soldiers, they will know we are near Saukenuk. We have no chance of attacking Fort Madison, or even the small fort at Prairie du Chien. We need more men. I have sent a messenger to Shabbona, who can go where we dare not. I have asked him to seek Tecumseh's brother, Neopope, who lives on the river below Rock Island, at a place named for him, 'Prophet's City.' He is feared and respected even among the Sioux. I have asked him to send word asking the Muscows, the Sioux, the Algonquins, and Winnebagos to join us in an attack on the whites."

"There is wisdom in that plan," Red Bird agreed. "But how much longer will you wait for word?"

"I promise that if we have not heard before the first frost, we will begin our raids."

Well within that month Shabbona arrived with his son, Matunuck, bringing good tidings. The Prophet had not failed. The whole Winnebago nation and the Algonquins had agreed to join Black Hawk. He was to begin a series of raids, at points as far away as possible, to make the white men think he had a much larger force than he did. At each raid, he was to leave some sign so the whites would know Black Hawk's braves had been there. Thus they could build up terror of Black Hawk even before his warriors were joined by the other nations.

Next dawn Red Bird set off with twenty-five warriors to Prairie La Crosse. There the farms were scattered across rolling hills, so it would not be easy for the whites to help each other.

"Try to bring back horses and grain," Black Hawk ordered.

Two dawns later, Naromse led a band of raiders to a farmhouse at a point where the Rock River joined the Mississippi. Just before the sun sank for the seventh time, both parties returned. They brought seven horses and fourteen scalps, but no grain. It had been destroyed by fire before the Sauks could rescue it. Black Hawk insisted on seeing every scalp to make certain his orders had been obeyed, and no woman or child was scalped.

The next sortie brought in four more horses and two young white women, who furnished much pleasure for the squaws, who took turns trying on camisoles, starched petticoats, stockings, and shoes. After the white girls realized they were safe from harm, they joined in the strange masquerade, donning the doeskin smocks and silver armbands of the squaws. They brought laughter to the little band of exiles, but they were no real substitute for grain.

"Singing Bird," Black Hawk called as he watched her cavorting about in the white girls' clothes, "I have a plan that will please you. Gather together twenty of the strongest squaws and maidens. We will take them to our cornfield, which we planted at the edge of the woods beyond the racing field. There we will harvest our own corn!"

Singing Bird was delighted.

"We will leave at dawn," Black Hawk said, "taking Naromse and five other braves who can ride, to carry the corn back on the broad backs of the horses. We will take fifteen braves on foot, lest there be trouble."

"There can be no bad trouble if we are together," she answered.

"Oh, Black Hawk, you do not know what it is like to be a squaw! Always waiting for a husband or a brother or a father to come home!"

For answer he tilted her chin up, as he used to, and touched her nose gently with his fingertip.

At sunrise the little party set out. As the new moon rode high above them, they tethered their horses. The braves took their positions around the field of gently waving corn tassels. The plants were heavily laden with the much-needed ears of sun-ripened corn.

Not a sound emerged from the cornfields as knives severed the ears from the plants and they were dropped into large goatskin bags. Bag after bag was filled under the very noses of the guards who patrolled the parapets of Saukenuk some five hundred paces distant. Each filled bag was passed from hand to waiting hand until it was grasped by one of the braves, who carried it to the horses. When the horses had all they could carry, the braves loaded the light canoe. The loading was almost completed when a running fox startled one of the horses. He whimpered in fright.

Black Hawk looked quickly toward Saukenuk and saw a dark silhouette run toward the nearest point of the parapet. The sound had been heard! The guard was joined by two others. Shots were fired from the parapet.

Bending low, he ran between the rows of corn to the nearest brave. "Tell them to hold their fire," he whispered. "The gun flashes will tell them where we are."

But his order came too late. An overeager young brave had fired at one of the figures on the parapet. The guard's rifle flew into the air, and he toppled backward off the high wall.

Naromse ran to Black Hawk's side. "The horses are farm horses, slow and heavy-footed."

"Leave them!" Black Hawk interrupted. "If they send out a sortie, they must use the South Gate. That will give you time to reach the foot trail leading to the plateau. Leave five men to guard the rear.

Tell them not to fire. Let the whites find the horses. That will delay them. If then they head toward the river, have our men decoy them into the forest by firing and with war whoops. We must get the squaws and the canoe-load of corn back to the lake."

Naromse was off, and Black Hawk turned to the figures crouching in the cornfield.

"Squaws and braves, follow me!" he cried, and ran toward the river. At the edge of the cornfield he paused to look back. Already Naromse's warriors were firing from the opposite edge of the field, where none of the little escaping force was to be found.

Then Singing Bird, carrying two heavily laden sacks of corn, one on each shoulder, caught up with him. "Take one of these," she whispered. "I'll race you to the canoes!"

So like the girl who once had raced him home from the plateau! He laughed aloud and took both bags from her and, running swiftly, reached the canoes before her. He dumped the bags into the stern, picked up his wife, and deposited her none too gently in the outrigger.

"Let that teach you not to boast," he said with mock sternness, and turned to count the others as they ran down the banks. When he was certain that all were safely aboard, he pushed the heavy outrigger off, and with the other braves plied his paddle, working the craft into deep water. The whole adventure was less like a battle than an escapade of naughty children raiding an apple orchard, yet according to the tales told of their great heroism against tremendous odds, the guards designated this exchange of shots as the first skirmish of the Black Hawk war!

Since the canoes had to be paddled against the current on the return journey, Naromse and his warriors reached the canoe cache first. Not a man had been lost, and none was wounded. True, they did not have the horses they had brought. But it was a happy little band that advanced toward the Lake of the Crying Geese.

As they broke from the woods and came into full view of the

lake, there was a sudden outcry, and a rider dashed toward them.

Both Black Hawk and Singing Bird recognized him.

"Loud Thunder!" Black Hawk cried.

"My son!" Singing Bird sobbed with happiness.

"I've come back." Loud Thunder addressed his father. "I want to fight by your side. A reservation in Iowa is no place for a true Sauk."

Naromse dropped his bags of corn and ran forward. "How did you get away?" he asked.

"Eleven of us took as many horses from the corral and left four dawns past," Loud Thunder answered.

"Eleven good Indian ponies! Now we can show them what a sortie should be!"

That same night Black Hawk told Shabbona of a plan that had been brewing in his mind on the return journey.

"The whites will know we are not with Keokuk when Loud Thunder's departure is reported. The time for action has arrived. If they know how small is our number of warriors, they will attack us at once. Nor will it take long for them to find us here. We must manage to make them believe we are many more than we are. We raid farmhouses at far distant points. But that is not enough. They must know that these raids are ours and not some marauding band of Chippewas. Whenever a raid is planned, you, with only Naromse or Matunuck, will mount two of the swiftest ponies. You will ride in advance of the raiders and warn the whites that Black Hawk and his terrible braves are about to attack."

"Why?" Shabbona asked, amazed.

"First, such a plan will build up a fear of Black Hawk and exaggerate the number of our men. Second, the whites will act on your warning and escape with their squaws and children to safety, and will leave the haymows and the grain lofts unprotected. We can seize the grain before setting torch to the farm. Thus we can have food for our own band for still another moon, and give the Prophet time to persuade other nations to join us."

"Are you sure this is not to avoid needless scalping of women and babies?" Shabbona asked, quizzically.

"No," Black Hawk admitted. "But it is a good plan, whatever the reason."

Five raids were planned for the following night, and at noon, Shabbona and his son rode off to warn the whites of the coming of Black Hawk's merciless band. And, when night fell, the five raiding parties found five deserted farms, with grain and other supplies awaiting the taking!

In the moons that followed, word spread like a forest fire. Black Hawk with countless men was on the warpath! The legend grew until Black Hawk became a mysterious and horrible figure, striking everywhere but never seen.

At last word came from the Prophet. The Osage had agreed to fight with the Sauk and the Fox. Shabbona had, by now, established himself as an Indian friendly to the whites. His warnings were talked of wherever white men met. The messenger from Neopope, the Prophet, brought word that he could safely pass among the Americans to consult with the Sioux.

"The Sioux will never be friendly to us!" Black Hawk exclaimed.

"The Prophet thinks they will," the messenger said. "The whites demanded part of their land. The Sioux ceded it to the government on condition that they might forever retain the plains where the buffalo herds feed. The Prophet has dreamed that the whites will break this promise. He told Chief Detroit that one day they would have to abandon all their land east of the Great Father of Many Waters. Detroit is so outraged he has agreed to join with you in an attack against the whites."

"Shabbona," Black Hawk said, "go with this brave. See Detroit if you can. Then go to Fort Madison and say that you wish to join the whites against us. They have spies who seek out our whereabouts, our plans. Why should there not be a spy for the Indians? If they really believe you are the white man's friend, they will welcome you. You can tell them anything about us. As long as the Osage, the Muscow, the Winnebago, and the Sioux will join us, we are safe in letting them think our forces are beyond counting."

"I will do it," Shabbona agreed.

"Remember, it would be well if any big encounter could await the coming of spring. Our raids have killed less than thirty whites, but we have struck terror in their hearts. We have food enough for many moons. We are safe unless our hiding place is found, which is unlikely, since it has not yet been discovered."

"If I cannot return, I'll send word, both of the whites' plans and our own," Shabbona said.

Upon his return, Shabbona reported he had been sworn in as a scout in the United States Army! He said he had told the whites he only pretended friendship with Black Hawk, but in truth he hated him and wanted him captured! He came now on a mission. He was to inform the Sauk Chief that militiamen were coming from Chicago by boat to join forces with the Army troops at Fort Madison and the fort at Prairie du Chien. Men would also come from the Army barracks at St. Louis. Their combined might would total many thousands. They would comb the forests and hunt down Black Hawk and his warriors.

"They want you to surrender," Shabbona ended.

"What news have you of Neopope?"

"He says you are to come with all your men at the next dark of the moon, that you are to use two hundred warriors to keep the troops at Fort Madison from joining the others and a hundred men to do the same at Prairie du Chien."

"That will leave less than fifty warriors to attack the men on the river!" Black Hawk exclaimed.

"He says you are to come downriver past Prophet Town till you reach a small scattering of houses. You and your party are to raid this village. But do not burn it, for the trees are leafless, and you may have to fight from the cover of the buildings."

"With less than fifty warriors?"

"The Sioux will attack the men on the Great Trail from St. Louis. The Winnebagos will take the covered bridge where the Great Trail crosses the river, ready to come to your aid should the attack be on the south bank, or go to help the Osage and the Muscows who will be on the northern shore waiting to repulse an attack in that direction."

"A dream come true at last!" Black Hawk cried. "Five Indian nations fighting side by side, united against the whites! We have little time to prepare. One of the raiding parties is still abroad. Why did you bring me such news so tardily?"

"I agreed to serve as messenger only on condition that I be not followed to your hiding place. Still I was followed. I backtracked and headed almost to the border of Canada. But I caught no glimpse of my pursuer. He was as wary as I."

"Think you it was an Army scout?"

"It could have been, or another Indian. There is a price on your head—a bounty—fifty silver dollars for you or any of your band. Dead or alive."

"Fifty silver dollars! The bounty on the fierce grizzly is but thirty-five! Who placed so generous a bounty?"

"The Great White Father in Washington—named Jackson. So the one who tried to follow might have been a seeker after gold. Or, perhaps, the brother of the two white maidens your men captured, who has sworn to avenge them."

"Are they so important to the whites that their safe return might be the basis of negotiations? I still only want Saukenuk returned to us. Would that be too large a ransom?"

"I will try," Shabbona replied. "If they agree, I shall return before the seventh day. So I must leave at once."

"Go, then, for it is our last chance to avoid much blood-spilling."

As he mounted his tired horse, Shabbona said, "Have your raiders capture two of what the whites call 'hayricks.' Fill them with stones and have your workhorses pull them to the gates of Fort Madison. Then cut the horses free." Seeing the wisdom of this plan, Black Hawk gave his approval, and Shabbona was off toward the Wide Trail.

Immediate preparations were begun for the biggest single sortie the Sauk and the Fox had made since Ashawequa. Late on the fifth night, the last raiding party returned. Black Hawk, awakened, sleepily watched the warriors dismount and unload the horses. He noticed three saddles. These must be captured horses, for the Sauks rode bareback. He saw, with satisfaction, eight rifles in the booty. Then he returned to his couch and slept.

At dawn when he rose and started to the lake to bathe, he noticed only two saddles hanging on the tree limbs. Had he not counted three the night before? He dismissed doubt from his mind and continued toward the lake. Barely had he reached its shore when a squaw came running from a tipi, crying, "The white maidens have gone!"

Then Black Hawk knew he had been right. There *had* been a third saddle. A hurried check showed only one horse missing. The spy must have ridden bareback and placed both girls on the saddled horse and joined the raiders without their knowledge.

Black Hawk changed plans without delay. Since their hiding place was now known to the whites, the squaws and old men could no longer be left there. Warriors could not be spared to guard them.

He called Walking Bear and issued orders to break camp immediately after they had gone. "Head the squaws to Four Lakes. Those of us who can will join you there after the battle. If the new camp remains undiscovered, we will make sorties from it as we have from here. If it is found, we shall, from now on, have to be encumbered with our families. But get them there in safety."

Black Hawk summoned Red Bird, Naromse, Loud Thunder, Matunuck, and the other chiefs.

"There is no longer reason to await Shabbona's return. The moon is but a sliver in the sky. If we are to get to our appointed posts by dark of moon, we must leave at once. Naromse, Matunuck, Loud Thunder, and five other braves, ride with my party. Red Bird and I will go afoot at the head of thirty-five warriors. We leave before the sun appears. Do your tasks well, for this sortie may well mean our return to Saukenuk. Watanka is with us. Remember, he smiles upon the followers of Black Hawk!"

CHAPTER 21

When Black Hawk's little band reached the settlement Shabbona had spoken of, it was apparent that the Shawnee chief had been there. Not a soul was in sight. Doors stood ajar. Belongings were scattered about. Even a few horses had been deserted in the frenzied flight of the white settlers. "Shabbona, the white man's friend," Black Hawk thought, and smiled.

There was no moon. The whites would not attack till morning, for the night gave the Indians too much advantage. Accompanied by Red Bird, Black Hawk scouted the scene of the coming battle and found it exactly as Shabbona had described it.

He looked across the river at the broad meadow that sloped upward to the forest. Few whites would be able to cross that open field if the Osage were behind those trees. But were they? There was no indication that any allies were near.

Where were the Winnebagos? Silently he and Red Bird crossed to the covered bridge. There was no sign that anyone had been there. Glancing downriver, he saw a large black form pushing its nose around the bend. The troops were arriving, but there were no allies!

Together he and Red Bird watched in fascinated horror as more and more of the boat appeared. Its great smokestack belched forth clouds of vapor; its paddles churned the water.

Black Hawk estimated that, at this rate, the steamboat would not reach the landing place till well after sunup. Seeing no sign of help, he ran back toward the woods where he had left his warriors.

"Loud Thunder," he ordered, "ride beside the Great Trail. Climb to a high hill and search the road. See if there is any sign of Dakota's

Sioux or of the enemy. Return quickly."

As his son leaped onto his pony and galloped along the deserted trail, Black Hawk turned to Red Bird. "If we have been betrayed, there is no time to send a runner to the fort. Even with stone blockades, two hundred braves cannot hold two thousand behind walls for long. They will be wiped out."

He saw that the boat was being moored to the landing platform. About four hundred men were crowded along its rails on two decks. Very soon they would disembark. He ran back to the woods as Loud Thunder dashed toward him.

"No Sioux in sight. But in the distance, many marching soldiers," he reported.

"We cannot retreat to the houses," Black Hawk said. "We would be caught there as snarling dogs tree a bear."

"We could try fleeing across the bridge," Red Bird suggested.

"To be shot down by the men on the dock as we run across the open meadow? No. We must surrender. The white flag, the flag of truce. Naromse, ride back to the empty houses. There are bits of white cloth in the windows. Bring one here. Quickly! All soldiers, everywhere, respect the white flag of surrender. It is the only way to save our warriors here and at the fort."

Men began pouring out onto the field from the riverbank. Then one, in the uniform of a Major, drew his sword and shouted, "Fifth Company, deploy!"

At the command, the militiamen spread out across the field, completely blocking any attempt to escape by way of the bridge. They lined up, row behind row, across the meadow and the road.

Black Hawk slashed a long branch from an ash tree, and as Naromse galloped up, seized the white muslin from his hand and knotted it around the stick.

"Naromse, Loud Thunder, Matunuck, take this. Ride to the center of the field. Stand there, holding the white flag high. When the major sends a man to talk, point back to us. Say, in English, 'Black Hawk give up!'"

There was a moment of complete silence as the three horsemen stood under the whipping white curtain. Then a shot rang out, and before Black Hawk's horrified gaze, Matunuck fell from his horse as only a dead man falls. Another shot, and Naromse's horse screamed and fell, throwing its rider. Loud Thunder flung the useless white emblem from him. Leaning down, he extended his hand to his fallen brother. Naromse grasped it and was jerked onto the horse behind Loud Thunder, who whirled and galloped toward the woods.

Black Hawk felt fury well up within him. He raised his long rifle and fired. He saw his bullet find its target. There was no time to reload. Turning, he shouted, "Shoot, and follow me."

Then the pent up rage burst from his lips in a scream as he raced out onto the field, wielding his rifle like a club, holding it by the barrel and swinging it like a deadly scythe. With angry cries, his warriors followed his example, wailing the long, drawn-out battle cry. The soldiers staggered back upon each other before the frenzied, furious attack.

"We're outnumbered!"

"Ambushed!"

"Sound retreat!"

The bugle did not sound because the bugler lay dead beside his crumpled instrument.

The men in the front ranks fell back against the men behind, who fell over the edge of the bank and down the slope onto the dock or into the water. Still Black Hawk pursued, his knife flashing and the dreadful musket swinging in its death-dealing arc. The soldiers scrambled up the gangplank, mauling each other in their frantic efforts to reach the safety of the troopship. But Black Hawk and Red Bird, side by side, pulled them from the slanting ramp and thrust them into the water.

"The bridge, Black Hawk," Red Bird cried. Black Hawk again called his men to follow. From the safe cover of the bridge, they had time to reload and pick off the soldiers as they climbed out of the water toward the gangplank. Then he remembered his men fighting against impossible odds at Fort Madison.

"Follow me!" he called and ran across the long bridge. As he heard the clatter of flying hoofs behind him, he called to his son.

"Loud Thunder, speed to the fort. Call off the warriors. Have them join me on the trail to Four Lakes."

And to Naromse, he said, "Go with him lest he is hurt and cannot get the message through."

Turning to the others, he commanded, "Run. Wait for us in the woods. Red Bird and I will cover you as you cross the field." But not a shot was fired. The longboat began to steam away ignominiously, leaving the dead in the water or on the bank to tell the shameful story of Stillman's Run.

As they walked back through the unmarked forest trail toward Four Lakes, Black Hawk's fury melted, leaving him weak and brooding.

"When I try to surrender, they will not let me, so much am I hated. The whites will stop at nothing till our nation is reduced to but a whisper in the wind. Watanka must frown upon me. I, who hate killing, seem doomed to fight, and to no avail."

The sun had scarcely reached the midmorning mark, when they heard the sound of hoofs and knew that their path met the wider trail from Fort Madison, and the warriors had overtaken them. They were jubilant, for not a man had been lost. Even Loud Thunder and Naromse, although saddened by the death of Matunuck, were filled with pride in their chieftain father. Black Hawk's thirty-eight braves standing at the side of the trail exchanged victorious shouts with the riders as they passed. But Black Hawk stood numb with grief and doubt.

Even so, he noticed a man on the very last horse. Covered

though the face was with the war paint of the Sauk, Black Hawk recognized Osauki. As the disguised white man saw the light of recognition in Black Hawk's eyes, he whipped the pistol from its holster. With weapon cocked, he aimed at Black Hawk's heart.

No word was spoken. The trigger finger tightened. The hammer fell. There was a click, but that was all. For a second time the white spy's gun had misfired. He let the pistol fall, staring in sheer amazement at his intended victim, so stunned that even when two braves leaped upon him, he did not defend himself.

A knife flashed upward. "Stop!" Black Hawk cried.

"He tried to kill you! He must die! He is a spy and would tell the whites the whereabouts of our camp."

"Release him!" Black Hawk commanded. Reluctantly the warriors obeyed.

"Not twice," Osauki murmured, staring at Black Hawk. "It couldn't happen twice without some reason. Black Hawk, I am beginning to believe. The Great Spirit must cherish you. For what purpose I do not know. Perhaps we are not meant to know. But this could not be chance. Let me live, and I shall be loyal all my days."

"I once said I would never die by your hand, Osauki," Black Hawk said. "You are the sign I needed to restore my own wavering faith. You are right. Such things do not happen twice by accident. There is a design we know not of, but now I can be sure that I am meant to go on with this seemingly senseless carnage."

Stooping, he picked up the fallen pistol and proffered it, butt end forward, to the white man. "Remount," he ordered. "Ride with my other loyal followers. There *is* cause for rejoicing, after all."

The camp at Four Lakes soon proved unsafe. In fewer than twenty dawns the Sauk and Fox warriors, with their squaws and children, were on the move. This was a period that seemed almost unbearable to Black Hawk. He had always loved the seeming permanence of Saukenuk. To have his people wandering from place to place seemed to him to lower the Sauk to a group of nomadic criminals.

The only thing that gave him courage to continue with raids and sorties was the hope that, by creating enough fear, they would force the whites to reconsider the terms of the old fraudulent treaty or make a new one allowing the return of Saukenuk to the Sauks.

Their camp on the Apple River was attacked by White Beaver, a Chippewa who had enlisted in the United States Army and been given charge of the war against the Sauk and the Fox. They moved on.

Again the Moon of Roses was upon them. There followed a series of skirmishes with both Indian and whites, with no decisive victory for either side. That these attacks did not result in a defeat of the Sauks was largely due to the advance knowledge furnished Black Hawk by Osauki.

Then on a morning in the Moon of Flying Pests, known to the whites as July, Osauki brought word that General Atkinson, in charge of the garrison at the fort at Prairie du Chien, had sent White Beaver and Colonel Winfield Scott, leading a combined force of white infantry against them. Black Hawk decided to move the whole encampment. Knowing how reluctant to shoot white men Osauki was, he placed the squaws and children under his care. He was to lead them across a shallow ford in the Bad Axe River, while the warriors met the attacking infantry at a point farther south.

Singing Bird pleaded with Black Hawk not to separate them, but he refused to heed her.

The two groups of Sauk and Fox left Apple River and headed for the shores of the Bad Axe. What neither Osauki nor Black Hawk knew was that General Atkinson, capitalizing on the ancient hatred between the two nations, had engaged a company of Sioux warriors to join in the attack, promising them that, if Black Hawk's forces were completely wiped out, the Sioux would be allowed to keep their remaining lands east of the Mississippi.

At first the great battle favored Black Hawk's warriors. The heavily wooded shores of the river provided the kind of terrain in which they were at their best, until the screaming Sioux were upon them, shooting, knifing, spearing, riding them down. The warriors were forced to give ground along the river's bank, retreating toward the shallower waters where the squaws were crossing. But the white soldiers closed around them, and Black Hawk saw that his whole pitiful struggle would be in vain.

At this point, Singing Bird disobeyed orders. She left the squaws and ran to the place where he and Red Bird were fighting. As she ran, she waved the white petticoat she had so long treasured.

"Black Hawk," she called, "surrender before we are lost."

"Go back!" he shouted.

Then he heard Red Bird groan. Blood came from his friend's mouth. Regardless of the hail of bullets, he dropped beside him, cradling him in his arms. Red Bird looked up.

"It's been good," he muttered. His eyes closed. Then Sioux, with scalping knives and tomahawks, were galloping toward them.

Black Hawk seized the white petticoat and waved it. No one gave heed. Then, a familiar sardonic voice spoke in his ear.

"Everything happens to you twice," Osauki said, as he fired a burst into the approaching Sioux. Even as they were falling, he slashed a strap from a horse and, seizing the saddle, ran with it over his arm. As he passed Singing Bird, he seized her arm.

"No!" she cried. "Let me stay with Black Hawk." But he dragged her toward the river.

It had turned a muddy crimson. Squaws with papooses on their backs were shot as they swam. Bodies floated downstream as logs in a millpond.

Osauki thrust Singing Bird into the water ahead of him and flung the saddle over her head and shoulders.

"Swim!" he ordered. Flinging himself in the water beside her, he rested his shotgun on the floating saddle. As he treaded water, he fired at white or Indian who aimed at them. He saw three white men fall and knew that he, Jeremiah Kilbourne, had killed those of his own race to protect an Indian squaw!

Next day, Black Hawk summoned his people—less than a hundred squaws and warriors—and told them he was going to give himself up.

"They will kill you!"

"We would rather follow you even if death awaits us. Do not leave us!"

"You can all be given protection," Black Hawk said. "I will demand it. Today, Black Hawk surrenders."

One of the squaws spoke up. "If you are to see the White Chief, you must not go in ragged chaps and bedraggled headdress. We, the squaws of the Sauk and the Fox, demand that you go as a proud warrior chieftain."

All that day the squaws toiled, and at last they had fashioned a fringed suit of bleached doeskin, with black beads sewn in the semblance of three tail feathers of the chicken hawk over the left breast. When Black Hawk lifted the flap of his tipi, dressed in the new garment, all exclaimed in admiration.

"Osauki, my son," Black Hawk said, "will you escort me to the barracks? Remove the war paint and red stain that covers your face and hands. You will go back to your own people as a white man."

"I'll not take you as a prisoner!" Osauki exclaimed. "If you think I'd collect the reward, you're mistaken!"

"You shall not have the silver, Osauki," Black Hawk said, smiling. "I am not your prisoner. You are my escort."

Black Hawk was handed over to White Beaver, who, in spite of Kilbourne's protests, ordered a heavy iron ball and chain fastened to the prisoner's leg.

"That is not done to prisoners of war!" a young officer cried.

"Besides being a prisoner of war, Lieutenant Davis," White Beaver replied, "Black Hawk has been arrested by the civil authorities."

"By whose order and on what charge?" Kilbourne demanded.

"On the order of General Atkinson. The charge is stealing corn."

In the custody of young Lieutenant Jefferson Davis, Black Hawk was sent by boat to the prison at Jeffersonville. Irked by the needless humiliation of his prisoner's ball and chain, Lieutenant Davis went out of his way to make things as easy as possible for him. The Sauk chieftain was constantly reminded of Davenport in the days when they had first met.

At first sight of his prison cell, Black Hawk wished a Sioux bullet had found his heart. But he remembered that Grey Owl, his brother, who had loved the freedom of forest and windswept plains as he did, had been confined for many moons in a room like this. So he forced himself to accept the confinement without protest.

CHAPTER 22

Black Hawk was not compelled to bear this confinement long, however. He was soon sent on a long journey throughout the eastern states.

"You must see the great power of the American government," he was told through the lips of the prison interpreter, "the iron road and the iron horses which we call 'railroads.' You must see our great buildings and get an idea what you are up against. You must be made to see the foolishness of revolting against progress."

But if that had been the purpose, why did they parade him, dragging his ball and chain, through the streets of Boston, Philadelphia, and Washington? Why were the crowds urged to gather and gape at the fallen hero? He knew! It was because he had dared to fight with the English whites against these whites. He and his small band had defied all this might for many years. Now he was being punished for his impertinence.

If they wanted to see a poor Indian humiliated in defeat, that's what he would give them! He remembered the pidgin English that Davenport had used in front of the two white men. And, although his face gave no indication of it, inwardly he smiled. So, when women standing below the platform upon which he was exhibited like a dancing bear would exclaim he "didn't look so terribly fierce," he would pound his chest obligingly.

"Me heap big Injun Chief," said the one-time Chief of All the Sauk and the Fox. He wished Davenport were there to hear him!

When he met Andrew Jackson in Washington, he felt he had never seen such hatred as flashed from the blue eyes under their bushy brows.

"Tell the Great White Father," Black Hawk said to the interpreter, "that Black Hawk thanks him for placing a higher value on him than on the fierce and dangerous grizzly bear!"

At the end of the tour, he was returned to his cell, which seemed welcome. Peace came to him there, as it had in the forests on the shore of the blue lake.

Then one morning the key turned in the lock, and the jailer opened the heavy iron door.

"Visitors," he said.

And there, in the large waiting room, were Singing Bird and Loud Thunder. For a moment no one spoke as they gazed upon each other, hungrily, searching for signs of illness or age. Black Hawk found that the old Indian squaw across the room was still the maiden who had shot a grouse he had missed!

"We've come to take you home," she said.

"Home?"

Her eyes fell.

"To Iowa, Father," Loud Thunder explained.

"Osauki paid for our coming here," Singing Bird said. "A man named Patterson and your friend Davenport have appealed many times to the Great White Father. They failed."

"Then who succeeded?"

"Keokuk."

"Keokuk obtained my release?"

"Where all the others failed, he succeeded."

Loud Thunder interrupted. "There is to be a big ceremony. You are to be welcomed back to your people. This will take place at the fort at the Prairie du Chien where you surrendered."

As Black Hawk, proudly bedecked in the white doeskin suit,

entered the crowded recreation room at the Fort, he saw White Beaver and General Atkinson seated at the head of the long council table, with Keokuk at the general's right. And then, as his eyes traveled around the room, he saw Davenport near the foot of the table. For the first time since his entrance, his eyes crinkled in what passed for a smile.

General Atkinson arose and beckoned him to come to the foot of the table.

"Black Hawk," he said, "we welcome you!"

He explained that, due to Keokuk's efforts, as well as his own, the Great White Father had agreed to the signing of a new treaty which granted the Sauk and the Fox nation certain lands in the state of Iowa with a generous amnesty, provided they remained within the confines of the reservation.

"Keokuk has already pressed his thumb upon the document. We ask for your thumbprint, too, that this treaty may become valid."

Black Hawk remembered another treaty which had been regarded as valid though it did not bear his thumb mark.

"You will sign now, without further delay," the general added impatiently. "You possibly are not aware that you have been released from prison, on probation, on the pleading of your Head Chief Keokuk. You are to be placed in his custody."

Black Hawk straightened up. He stood for a moment, staring in disbelief. Then, as Keokuk arose in his place, as if about to speak, Black Hawk turned and walked in silence toward the door.

"Black Hawk!"

It was the voice of Davenport that stopped him. He looked at his old friend.

"Have I the general's permission to speak to this man?" Davenport said, addressing Atkinson. "I have known him for many years. I may have some influence with him."

"Go ahead."

Before Davenport could speak, Keokuk, growling fiercely, said in Sauk, "I demand an apology."

"Don't crowd your luck, Keokuk," Davenport said, also in Sauk. Turning to Black Hawk, he said, "Black Hawk, do you remember our mutual friend, Running Deer? I wish he were here now that I might talk to you through him. Trust me. This is the best way. Sign the document. It will be better for your people and for you.

"Do you recall a conversation we once had while sitting in a canoe? About the Davenport House? What was said then is now true. If the conditions elsewhere are unpleasant, you and Singing Bird are welcome always."

Suddenly Black Hawk's eyes glowed, and he nodded.

"Tell them I apologize for my rude behavior to the mighty warrior, Keokuk," he said. "And that Black Hawk will sign."

The white interpreter whispered so that his voice would not be overheard by Keokuk. "Shall I say it just that way or may I be nice about it?" he asked, and grinned in warm friendliness.

After the meeting, when people were standing about in little groups, Black Hawk sought out the interpreter.

"Your name is La Clare, I am told," he said.

"Yes, I am the official interpreter for the Sauk Reservation. I think you guessed I'm not too fond of your new boss."

"Mr. La Clare," Black Hawk said, "do you know a man named J. B. Patterson?"

"I do. He and his son publish a paper in Iowa near the reservation."

"Mr. La Clare, I shall, I hope, see a great deal of you. Find Patterson. There is something I should like to talk of with both of you."

Black Hawk sat on the little veranda of the Davenport House and self-consciously held his wife's hand where it rested on his shoulder. Singing Bird, equally uncomfortable, stared straight ahead with grim and deadly fixity. On the ground in front of them, his head hidden by a black cloth, stood Colonel George Davenport. He was taking their picture with a newfangled device invented by a Frenchman named Daguerre.

His head appeared from under the cloth. "I suppose it would be too much if I asked you both to smile," he said almost plaintively. He disappeared under the black cloth and looked in the "finder" but could discover no noticeable change of expression. Resignedly, he pressed the bulb.

"Now relax. Future generations will know what you looked like, and your friends can have something to remember you by."

Three years had passed since their last meeting. The whites had again broken their promise, and Keokuk had been asked to move the remnant of the once powerful Sauk and Fox nation from Iowa to Oklahoma. Black Hawk could not face the thought of the added humiliation of a move to unfamiliar surroundings. He had asked Antoine La Clare to write Davenport to ask if the invitation he had extended in Black Hawk's darkest hour still held. Within three days they had not only the cordial affirmation, but the transportation money had been forthcoming.

"There was no need to ask," Davenport said when he met their steamer. "I once told you I'd bought the place for you. It's yours for as long as you live." He seated himself opposite them in the carriage and signaled the driver to proceed.

"I want to die here," Black Hawk said. "I want to be buried here, too. Will you have them seat us side by side below the back veranda where we can see both the apple blossoms and the river?"

Davenport nodded.

"Have them build a small house of logs over us," Black Hawk continued. "When the logs rot and crumble, no one will know where we are. That is as I wish it."

"I too should like that," Singing Bird added quietly.

Now as they sat on their veranda that faced the river, Black Hawk's eyes were narrowed.

"Keokuk, the White Man's Friend," he said softly, after a long silence. "He tried by compromise to save our nation. I tried by fighting. We both have failed. We both wanted only to be let alone. But that was asking the impossible. No nation can any longer live alone. Its neighbors are too close. And no strong neighbor gives help to a weak one. Only the strong can demand help in time of trouble."

He lapsed into silence, and the paled autumn sun poured down upon his calm face. Presently he spoke again.

"Keokuk already has a statue erected in his honor. He sits on his great horse, and no one will ever guess that he was so short. You have had a city named for you, my friend. But men still might not know of the fine man, the loyal friend, from whom it was named."

He stood up, and looking down at Davenport, his eyes crinkled as he smiled.

"Why couldn't you have done that when I was taking your picture?" Davenport complained good-naturedly.

"Because now I am thinking that I shall make all of us live forever. *I* have written a book."

"You have!" his friend exclaimed incredulously.

"Antoine La Clare translated it, and it was edited by my old friend, J. B. Patterson. It is not a very good book," Black Hawk added modestly.

"It is good," Singing Bird said indignantly. "La Clare read it to us."

"It is full of words," Black Hawk continued, "and whether it is good or not good, it is the words that matter. For words are like the pollen of the wild rose. Wherever they are blown, a seed is planted."

"That's fine, Black Hawk," Davenport applauded. "It's high time someone told the truth about the shameful injustices heaped by my people upon yours."

Black Hawk nodded. "Perhaps someday someone will read my words and want to help my people. I would like to think that, but I do not. We were in the way. We were conquered, not by your people, but by words and ideas. It seems to me I have always known that was how it would be. That was why I always wanted words to speak with. Now I have them, and they are printed in a book for all to read."

He smiled down at his old friend. "Someday someone will read them and say, 'Black Hawk, him heap smart Injun, huh?'"

Davenport looked up at him and grinned. "Huh," he said.

Appendix

To: Brigadier Gen'l H. Atkinson

Sir—

The changes of fortune, and vicissitudes of war, made you my conqueror. When my last resources were exhausted, my warriors worn down with long and toilsome marches, we yielded and I became your prisoner.

The story of my life is told in the following pages; it is intimately connected, and in some measure identified with a part of the history of your own: I have, therefore, dedicated it to you.

The changes of many summers, have brought old age upon me,—and I cannot expect to survive many moons. Before I set out on my journey to the land of my fathers, I have determined to give my motives and reasons for my former hostilities to the whites, and to vindicate my character from misrepresentation. The kindness I received from you whilst a prisoner of war, assures me that you will vouch for the facts contained in my narrative, so far as they came under your observation.

I am now an obscure member of a nation that formerly honored and respected my opinion. The path to glory is rough, and many gloomy hours obscure it. May the Great Spirit shed light on yours—and that you may never experience the humility that the power of the American government has reduced me to, is the wish of him, who, in his native forests, was once as proud and bold as yourself.

—BLACK HAWK

Month of the Falling Leaves, 1833

Bibliography

Autobiography of Ma-Ka-Tai-me-she-kia-kiak (or Black Hawk). Antoine La Clare, U.S. interpreter. J. B. Patterson, editor and amanuensis. Continental Printing Co., 1882.

Beals, Frank Lee, Chief Black Hawk. Wheeler, Chicago, 1943.

Black Hawk. Edited by Donald Jackson. University of Illinois Press, 1955-56.

Black Hawk, The Man—The Hero—The Patriot. Annals of Iowa, 1895-97, pp. 450-464.

Bloom, Margaret, Black Hawk's Trail. A. Whitman & Co., Chicago, 1936.

Bryan, William Smith, and Rose, Robert, Black Hawk. Bryan Beard & Co, St. Louis, 1876.

Cole, Cyrus, I Am a Man: the Indian Black Hawk. State Historical Society of Iowa, 1938.

Derleth, August William, Wind over Wisconsin. C. Scribner's Sons, New York, 1939.

Drake, Beryan, Life and Adventures of Black Hawk. H. M. Rulenson, 1856.

Life of Black Hawk. Edited by Milton Quaife. Donelly & Sons Company, Chicago, 1916.

Life of Black Hawk. State Historical Society of Iowa, 1932.

Meese, William A., Upper Mississippi Sketches. Moline, Illinois, 1904.

Monahan, Jay, Black Hawk Rides Again. Wisconsin Magazine of History, Madison, 1945.

Smith, Elbert H., History of Black Hawk. Milwaukee, 1846.

Stevens, Frank E., The Black Hawk War. Frank E. Stevens, Chicago, 1903.

Stocking, Amer Mills, The Saukie Indians and Their Great Chiefs Black Hawk and Keokuk. The Vaile Co., 1926.